"You've seen them disappear, too," she whispered. "You saw what I saw."

"I didn't know what you'd seen," he finally said. "I . . . I wondered."

"Who are they?" she asked. "How can they . . ."

"I used to call them the Remarkables," Charley said. "When I first found them."

His voice came out sounding strangely bitter, even though the words sounded nice. It was like biting into a cookie and discovering it was flavored with pepper instead of chocolate.

"Remarkables?" Marin repeated.

Also by Margaret Peterson Haddix

MARGARET PETERSON HADDIX

REMARKABLES

KATHERINE TEGEN BOOKS
An Imprint of HarperCollins Publishers

Katherine Tegen Books is an imprint of HarperCollins Publishers.

Remarkables

Copyright © 2019 by Margaret Peterson Haddix

All rights reserved. Printed in the United States of America.

No part of this book may be used or reproduced in any manner whatsoever without written permission except in the case of brief quotations embodied in critical articles and reviews. For information address HarperCollins Children's Books, a division of HarperCollins Publishers, 195 Broadway, New York, NY 10007.

www.harpercollinschildrens.com

Library of Congress Control Number: 2019000073
ISBN 978-0-06-283847-6

Typography by David Curtis
20 21 22 23 24   PC/BRR   10 9 8 7 6 5 4 3 2 1

First paperback edition, 2020

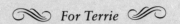 *For Terrie*

ONE

Marin stared at the towering wall of cardboard boxes that ran down the middle of her family's new living room. It was like something out of a fairy tale—it seemed like every time she or Dad moved or unpacked one box, another one grew in its place.

Dad reached over to give her ponytail a playful tug.

"Here's the game plan, kiddo," he said. "We do two more boxes, then we take a break. A *well-deserved* break."

"But we told Mom—" Marin began.

A sudden, furious cry sounded from upstairs. Dad threw his arms up in the air as if someone had scored a touchdown.

"Yes!" Dad said. He did a little victory dance. Dad was a gym teacher—he was good at victory dances. "Baby Owen thinks it's break time *now*."

"I'll get him," Marin volunteered, scrambling up and jumping over a lampshade and a long sheet of Bubble Wrap that hung half in, half out of the box in front of her.

"You just want to leave me to deal with . . . more pillows? Why do we have all these pillows?" Dad asked, staring down in mock dismay at the box he'd just opened on the floor before him.

Marin giggled and took the stairs two at a time, almost smacking into the wall. She wasn't used to a staircase that bent in the middle yet. Their house back in Illinois had had stairs that just went straight up and down. Sometimes when Mom and Dad weren't looking, she and Kenner and Ashlyn used to sit on a blanket on the top step and shove off and then . . .

Stop thinking about Kenner and Ashlyn, Marin told herself.

She turned the corner into her baby brother's room. His cries were louder now; it was amazing that such a tiny creature could make so much noise.

"Shh, shh," Marin murmured, just like she'd heard Mom and Dad do. "I'm here, Owen. Did you think we'd left you all alone?"

That word, *alone,* stuck in her throat a little.

She took three steps to her brother's crib, which was the only furniture in the room so far. The pieces of the changing table lay on the floor, waiting for her and Dad to put it together. Owen's cries echoed off bare walls.

"Are you hungry?" Marin asked, peeking over the crib railing. "Or just mad? Or do you have a dirty diaper?"

Owen's cries turned into more of a snuffling sound as he

peered up at her. Tears trembled in his eyelashes.

Marin still wasn't used to having a baby brother. She'd had eleven years to get used to being an only child, and only eight weeks to get used to being a big sister.

And Owen was so tiny and helpless. His miniature hands swiped the air as if he hadn't figured out how they worked yet. His face was red with crying, and his lips quivered. But his dark eyes tracked Marin's movements as she reached down to slide her hand under the back of his *Play Ball!* T-shirt and lift him up.

Mom and Dad said Owen looked and acted almost exactly like Marin had when she'd been his age.

"Don't be like me," Marin whispered. "Be better. Make Mom and Dad proud."

TWO

"This is one of the greatest things about having a new baby in the family," Dad told Marin as he settled into the couch with Owen in his arms. "Baby on my lap, bottle in his mouth, ESPN on TV . . . When you were a baby, your mother and I used to fight over whose turn it was to feed you. Of course, she almost always won. Home court advantage, you could say. But now . . ." Dad winked. "Don't tell your mother, but I'm kind of glad she has to work so much right now."

Dad meant that when Mom was around, she didn't need a bottle to feed Owen. Even now, the milk Owen was drinking came from her. She'd pumped it just that morning before leaving for her new job.

Dad patted the couch cushion beside him.

"Join us," he told Marin. "We can have a three-fourths-of-the-Pluckett-family cuddle. It's just about time for the baseball bloopers reel from the weekend."

Dad loved blooper reels from any sport. He always looked

for the dumbest mistakes professional athletes made so he could show his gym classes whenever he introduced a new sport.

"Look at that!" he'd say. "That guy is making millions of dollars a year playing soccer, and he *still* kicked the ball into the wrong goal! So don't worry about doing this wrong, kids! You could *never* mess up as badly as the pros!"

Marin wasn't in the mood to watch people making mistakes.

"I think I'll go outside for a little bit," she said. "Explore the backyard, since it was too dark last night."

"Good choice!" Dad nodded enthusiastically. He clunked his forehead with the hand that wasn't supporting Owen's head. "What kind of a dad—or phys ed teacher—am I that I didn't suggest that? Of *course* you should go outside and play! Get some fresh air! Go! Just do it!"

Back in Illinois, Kenner had said to Marin once, "Is your dad ever anything but loud? Does he ever stop being a gym teacher?"

And Ashlyn had giggled in a way that somehow wasn't very friendly, even though Marin and Ashlyn had been friends practically their whole lives.

"It's like Marin's dad is just one big puppy dog," she said.

How was it possible to make a puppy dog sound like a problem? Like something to be ashamed of?

Kenner and Ashlyn aren't here, Marin told herself. *They're back in Illinois. I live in Pennsylvania now. I'll probably never see them again in my entire life.*

She slid open the glass door that separated the far end of the family room from the brick patio outside. The side of the patio was lined with three huge bushes, and all three were in different stages of blooming: one with the remains of dried-up yellow blossoms, one with purple flowers at their peak, and one with thick glossy leaves and just the start of dignified white flowers.

Forsythia, lilac, rhododendron, Marin said to herself. She liked knowing the names of things.

She stepped out and shut the door behind her, and that was enough to silence the cheering from Dad's TV.

Back in Illinois, their backyard had been small and flat and square. Every year at Easter, Dad always complained that there was no good place to hide eggs, because everything was out in the open. Mom always teased, "Don't you just mean, Marin's better at finding things than you are at hiding them? Come on, can't you admit that your daughter is smarter than you are?" It was kind of a little routine they had.

This backyard looked like it'd be a great place to hide *anything*. Maybe even another house. Only a small strip of grass lay beyond the patio, and then the yard sloped up and turned into an expanse of wildflowers and brambles and gently swaying trees. It was like their own private family woods. Marin couldn't even see through it to tell what lay on the other side.

If I have a bad day at school here, I'll be able to come home and step out into those woods and shut it all out, Marin thought. *Nobody will know if I'm crying.*

One of the sprigs of lilac blew against her arm, as if to remind her she wasn't in Illinois anymore. The lilac blooms had already withered back in Illinois.

I'm not going to have bad days at school here, Marin told herself firmly. *I won't have any reason to cry.*

Marin walked over to the edge of the woods. Up close, she found that the undergrowth had gaps she hadn't seen from the patio. And one of the gaps turned into a narrow, pebble-covered path that wound back through the trees.

"It's our yard. I belong here," Marin said out loud, as if someone might be watching in disapproval.

She stepped onto the path. Vines brushed against her bare legs, and when she looked down, she saw that little prickly bristles had already embedded themselves into the shoelaces of her sneakers.

No one was watching her. She bent down and split open one of the bristles to find the seed inside. Mr. Wu, her fifth-grade science teacher back in Illinois, had been right.

"Aren't plants brilliant?" he'd raved, waving his arms joyously in front of the Smartboard image of all sorts of bristles and burrs. "Plants can't walk around, so they pack up their seeds in little containers, and send them out on creatures that can walk. Like *us*."

Kenner had made fun of Mr. Wu the same way she made fun of Marin's dad. Kenner said Mr. Wu spiked his hair up too much. And Ms. Condi, their language arts teacher, didn't know how to put on makeup, and Mr. Stewart, the social studies teacher, had bad breath, and . . .

Marin took off running deeper into the woods. Even though it was a sunny June day, the light dimmed under the trees. This would definitely be a good place to hide, if Marin ever needed one.

I won't need that here, she told herself, in time with the sound of her feet hitting the ground. *I won't. I won't. I won't.*

And then Marin reached the end of the woods.

THREE

Marin *knew* that their new house was at the top of a hill. She knew that their new town was called Summitview, and that the road that led to their neighborhood circled up and up and up, higher and higher.

But knowing that was one thing. Looking down on an entire town was something else.

The roofs of some of her neighbors' houses were beneath her. The tops of church steeples were beneath her. The clock tower of the county courthouse was beneath her.

It wasn't exactly all easy to see, because the house directly behind the woods was in the way. And suddenly, Marin wanted to see everything. If only she was a little taller. Or—

Marin looked up. The tree beside her was a huge maple, with thick branches that started right above her head and went up like a ladder. The tree rose so far up into the sky that she couldn't see the top.

This was an excellent tree for climbing.

Marin reached for the lowest branch, and swung and flipped her body around until she could wrap a leg around the branch, too. It would have been good if she'd been wearing jeans instead of flimsy running shorts, because the bark scratched her legs. But she managed to hoist herself up, so in just a matter of minutes she was standing on the lowest branch. Then she stepped up to the next and the next and the next.

When she was about twenty feet above the ground—and hundreds of feet above the main part of her new town—Marin reached a gap in the branches. Now she had a clear view. The town in the valley below looked like a doll village, or maybe one of the scenes her grandfather built for his model railroads. But the sun was in her eyes when she gazed in that direction. It was easier to look down at the houses closest to the edge of the woods, where the glow was more subtle. The roof of the nearest house, right past Marin's toes, almost seemed to shimmer.

"Race you!" someone called below.

"It's too hot for that! I concede! You win!" someone else laughingly called back.

Marin tightened her grip on the thick center branch of the tree and ducked her head behind a clump of maple leaves. She didn't want anyone seeing her. It would be too hard to explain why she was in the tree, and that she really wasn't spying. It was hard enough to think of saying, "Hi, I'm Marin.

I'm your new neighbor." She could hear Kenner's voice in her head, the way Kenner complained when Marin didn't want to talk much: *Why do you always have to act so weird? What's wrong with you?*

But Marin *was* curious about who was down below. She inched her face ever so slightly to the side, peeking out again past the leaves.

A pack of kids had just turned the corner onto the street that stretched out before her, leading up the hill toward the woods. They all looked older than Marin—one of the boys actually had a curly beard shadowing his jawline.

Teenagers, Marin decided. She took note of the back-packs sagging from their shoulders, some decorated with rainbow-colored duct tape or leopard-print ribbons or cam-ouflage patches. She remembered Mom texting pictures of Summitview when she'd come out ahead of the rest of the family to house hunt, and how she'd narrated, "And this is the high school, which is actually walking distance from the house I like best. . . . Marin, for middle school, you'll have to take a bus, but after that, it would just be a short walk. . . ."

These teenagers were coming home from school. Even though Marin had had *her* last day of school two weeks ago back in Illinois, the school year went later here in Pennsylvania.

None of the teenagers tilted their heads up toward Marin's

tree. She dared to peek out a little more.

One of the girls had a hand resting on the shoulder of one of the guys; one of the other girls was braiding another girl's hair, even as they walked. One of the boys bounced a basketball back and forth with everyone else, with all the others taking turns. And they all looked . . .

Happy, Marin thought. *No, not just that. They're happy together.*

These kids might as well have been an alien species. Marin had never really known any teenagers well. Neither she nor Ashlyn nor Kenner had older brothers or sisters. And when Mom and Dad wanted to get a babysitter and go out somewhere without her on a Friday or Saturday night, they always made arrangements with friends.

Mom and Dad had a lot of friends. Marin was pretty sure they'd both had a lot of friends their entire lives. They weren't like she'd been in fifth grade, watching the other friend groups on the playground and wondering, *How is it that Amirah and Sadie are best friends, when Amirah sits and draws all the time, and Sadie is constantly in motion? What do Stana and Alex whisper about all the time? What happened, that Josie and Emma stopped being friends on a Monday and were friends again by Wednesday and then not friends ever again after Friday?*

Now Marin watched the teenagers, and Kenner wasn't

here to say, *What are you doing? Why are you staring like that? You look so weird!*

The squad of teenagers reached a portion of their street where the pavement turned sharply uphill. It was clear they were used to the dramatic incline, because none of them slowed down. One of them—a girl with tangled red curls and a yellow skirt that flowed around her knees like sunbeams—even turned around, so she climbed the hill backward while she kept up a conversation with the kids behind and below her.

When the group was about halfway up the hill, a battered old car spun around the corner at the bottom of the street. Even more teenagers leaned out the side windows, one of them jokingly taunting, "Oh, did you leave early so you could get the snacks ready for us?"

"No, we just didn't have to wait in the line of gas-guzzling cars!" the red-haired girl retorted. "We were more environmental and healthier and"—she raised her face to the sky—"we got to enjoy the nice weather!"

She spun completely around, her skirt flaring out. From above, with her bright hair and swirling skirt, she looked like a kindergartener's drawing of the sun.

"Yes, but we . . ." The boy in the car dropped his voice. Marin leaned closer, but she couldn't hear what he said.

The car putt-putted on up the street to the last house, the one closest to Marin's tree. Three boys and a girl climbed out. The girl and one of the boys began an old-fashioned dance—a waltz, maybe?—on the yard while they waited for the walkers to catch up.

Was this the beginning of a party? For all Marin knew, maybe high school kids had parties every day after school.

Or were they all brothers and sisters? Did every single one of those teenagers live in the same house?

Marin decided she had brothers and sisters on her mind just because of having a new brother herself. The nine teenagers would have had to include multiple sets of twins or triplets, to have that many siblings so close in age. And they didn't look anything alike—some were short and some were tall; some were bony-thin and some were comfortably padded. Also, their noses and eyes and mouth shapes were all different; they had a wide range of hair colors and skin tones. It made Marin think of first-grade art class, when the teacher had held up a fistful of different crayons and said, "Draw your self-portrait however you want! Show me how you see yourself!"

It had to be that these teenagers were just a bunch of friends. But Marin kept thinking they acted more like family.

Maybe some or all of them were adopted. Maybe they were foster brothers and sisters.

Marin blinked, trying to figure it out.

And in that one instant, every single one of the nine teenagers vanished.

FOUR

Marin almost fell out of the tree in surprise. Then she leaned so far out looking for the missing teenagers that she could only use one hand to hold on to the center branch. Her fingers slipped across the bark. She had to dig in her fingernails to stay in place.

She blinked again, once, then twice. Had something suddenly gone wrong with her eyes—something that could be fixed by squeezing her eyelids shut and then opening them again?

The grass and sidewalk and driveway where the nine teenagers had stood and danced and milled about only a moment earlier stayed empty. If she squinted ever so slightly, Marin could make out individual blades of grass; she could see tiny cracks in the pavement. Her eyes were fine. So it was impossible that she could suddenly miss seeing nine teenagers.

Had she only imagined them in the first place?

That was a crazier thought. The car was still parked

crookedly in the driveway, practically within spitting distance of Marin high up in her tree. She could hear the little clicking noise that some car engines made, cooling off. That car *hadn't* been there when Marin had first climbed the tree. She had definitely seen the teenagers drive it up the hill and park it and get out and dance and—and . . .

Disappear.

This isn't real, Marin thought. *That's not how the world works. People aren't here one minute and gone the next without leaving a trace.*

At least, that wasn't how the world had ever seemed to work before. Not ever before in Marin's entire life.

But we lived in Illinois before, and now . . .

That was crazy, too. It wasn't like Pennsylvania was *that* different from Illinois, that people here could just vanish at will.

If nothing else, Mom and Dad would have warned Marin about that change.

Marin held back a giggle, because she had a feeling that if she started to giggle, she wouldn't be able to stop. It might turn into hysteria. And it probably wasn't a good idea to go into hysterics twenty feet off the ground, holding on to a tree branch with only one hand—or, really, with only four fingernails dug into the bark.

Down below, someone laughed.

Marin jerked again in surprise, coming even closer to

falling. Her pinkie slid off the bark, so now she was holding on with only three fingernails.

Marin grabbed a new branch with her other hand and stepped a little farther out so she could look through a different gap in the leaves. She needed a different angle, because the laughter hadn't come from the front yard of the teenagers' house.

It had come from the back.

Marin ducked down, gazing past the roof of the single-story house—past the mossy green shingles and the weathered gray gutters and downspouts.

And there, at the back of the house, was a huge patio shaded by the trees. All nine of the teenagers who had vanished from the front yard were now draped over the patio furniture in the back—five kids sprawled over the benches of a long picnic table, four lolling in lounge chairs padded with cushions covered with huge tropical flower prints in bright oranges and greens.

It was the red-haired girl who'd laughed.

"Homework time, remember?" one of the other girls said, her voice a mix of sternness and affection.

"I know, I know," the red-haired girl said, her laughter still bubbling over. Marin decided this girl's name should be Sunshine, or Sunny, or something like that. "It's just . . . sometimes calculus *is* funny."

The other girl grinned and nodded, and they all bent their heads over books and calculators again. They munched grapes and carrots and handfuls of popcorn, but stayed intent on their work.

It was an ordinary scene—well, except for the fact that nine kids could do homework together so quietly. But maybe that was a skill kids acquired once they got to high school. And maybe the high school level was when math got funny— none of Marin's teachers had ever acted like there was any humor in it. But the way the teenagers all sat so calmly now made Marin doubt even more what she'd seen before. Or . . . not seen.

Maybe when Marin blinked that first time, she'd had her eyes shut longer than she thought. Maybe it had been long enough for every single one of the teenagers to walk from the front yard into the house and then out the back.

That wasn't a blink. That was practically a *nap*. Or the amount of time Marin kept her eyes shut when she used to play hide-and-seek and she was It, and she had to count to a hundred before she opened them.

Marin hadn't counted at all, a moment ago. She truly had only blinked. And even if all nine teenagers had run as fast as they could, they hadn't had time to scramble out of sight and into the backyard that quickly.

So was it . . . magic? Marin wondered. *Or . . . what's it called . . . teleporting?*

"Mar-in!" she heard Dad call, far off in the distance. She could tell he was doing his whisper-yell. Owen must have fallen asleep again, and Dad was trying not to wake him. It was an amazing skill Dad had, that she'd never known about until eight weeks ago when Owen was born.

Down below, none of the teenagers looked up or turned their heads toward Dad's voice. Maybe they were all just very focused on their homework. But what if they *couldn't* hear Dad? What would that mean?

Marin couldn't come up with a possibility that explained any of it. She was suddenly too spooked to think clearly. Something really weird was going on here—what if it was something really dangerous, too?

Marin scrambled down from the tree as quickly and quietly as she could. She didn't want any of the teenagers to know she was there. She didn't want any of them chasing her.

As soon as she hit the ground, she took off running back to Dad, as fast as her legs would carry her.

FIVE

"Amazing," Mom said.

It was evening now, and Mom was home from work. Mom was standing before the somewhat smaller wall of boxes in the living room, which Marin and Dad had worked on steadily for the rest of the afternoon.

Marin had not told Mom anything about the teenagers in the house behind the woods, or the way they'd seemed to disappear from their front yard and reappear in the back.

She hadn't told Dad, either.

It hadn't felt like she could, once she'd gotten back to her own house, with the car commercials on ESPN in the background, and Owen's bottle rinsed out and drying in the rack by the sink, and Dad so hearty and gung ho about starting on the next layer of boxes. Once everything was ordinary again, it was even harder to believe that she'd seen something extraordinary.

But Marin had thought about the teenagers all afternoon,

distractedly muttering, "Uh-huh," or "Hunh-uh," as Dad chattered on and on and Owen woke and ate and slept and woke and ate and slept again.

"I know what you mean!" Dad said excitedly to Mom now, as he gestured at the remaining boxes. "At daybreak this morning, I thought that pile of boxes was like the Great Wall of China, and they'd be there for thousands of years. But now I'm thinking it's more like the Berlin Wall. Thirty years, tops, we'll have that baby taken care of. Don't you see the line of East German cars on the other side, waiting to drive through to freedom?"

Mom laughed and ruffled Marin's hair.

"Was Dad regaling you with history references all afternoon? Practicing?"

"Mmm," Marin said, because she couldn't really remember what Dad had said.

That was apparently enough of an answer for Mom, because now she was hugging Dad, and reaching out to draw Marin into the hug.

"You'll find a job," Mom told Dad.

Marin knew everything her parents were skipping over and not saying, because they'd already said it a hundred times. The Plucketts had moved to Pennsylvania because of Mom's job. When Marin was really little, Mom had been a nurse working the night shift so Dad could work days, and

Marin always had at least one parent home with her. Then, when Marin started school, Mom switched to teaching other nurses so she could have her evenings free, when Marin was home. Evidently she was really, really good at her job, because a small nursing school Mom had never even heard of in Pennsylvania had heard about her, and asked her to be their dean and redesign their entire program.

Mom had been all ready to tell the college no—"I'm six months pregnant! I'm about to go out on maternity leave! The timing is impossible!" But Dad had said, "Isn't this your dream job? And if they really want you, don't you think they'll work out the logistics?"

Dad's job was the only problem that hadn't worked out yet. As in, he wasn't sure if anyone in Pennsylvania would hire him. Most schools only had one gym teacher, so he thought his best hope was probably teaching social studies— something he hadn't done since his student teaching days in college.

Secretly, Marin thought Kenner was kind of right about Dad: Even as a social studies teacher, he would still sound like a gym teacher. He'd probably make everything into a game—history baseball, maybe; geography races. . . .

But wouldn't that make social studies more fun? Marin thought loyally. *So there, Kenner!*

It was crazy to be saying "So there!" to Kenner in her

mind, from hundreds of miles away, when she'd never been able to say that to Kenner in person.

It was crazy to even think about Kenner when Marin was never going to see her again.

Marin burrowed deeper into the hug with Mom and Dad.

"Even if I have to sub for a year or two, that's fine," Dad said, resting his chin on Mom's head and a hand on Marin's back, drawing her closer. "It might even work better, with the baby. More flexibility."

Marin knew what Dad wasn't saying, too: Substitute teachers didn't make as much money as other teachers.

"I'm so lucky to have such a supportive family!" Mom exclaimed. "Marin, you've been such a trooper, too. I don't think I've heard you complain once about leaving all your friends behind. . . ."

Marin was glad her face was buried between Dad's T-shirt and Mom's silky blouse, so no one could see her guilty expression. She lifted her head just a little and peeked up, to see if she was going to have to answer, but Mom had moved on. She was brushing a lock of her short sandy hair out of her face and sniffing the air.

"And did you two already fix dinner? Is that *lasagna* I smell?" Mom asked.

The air *did* smell like lasagna, even though Marin knew for a fact that the kitchen was still in disarray, and the closest thing to cooking either she or Dad had done was warming up Owen's bottles.

Dad was sniffing, too.

"Sorry—you must be smelling a neighbor's dinner," he told Mom. "Too many open windows, I guess. I was planning to order pizza, but . . ."

Just then, the doorbell rang.

"That was fast, considering I haven't even *called* for pizza yet," Dad said, joking again. "Or figured out where the nearest delivery place is. Ooh, maybe it's Girl Scout cookies. I could eat nothing but Girl Scout cookies tonight and go to bed, and be perfectly happy."

Mom laughed and went for the door. She opened it to reveal a woman standing on the porch with a picnic basket and something in a tinfoil tray.

"Welcome to the neighborhood!" the woman said. "I'm Mrs. Jean Schmidt from next door."

Dad winked at Marin.

"Whoever that woman is, she's already my favorite neighbor if there's lasagna in that tray," he whispered. "And if she wants to be called Mrs. Jean Schmidt, I'm never calling her anything else."

Dad joined Mom by the door, and he pulled Marin over to say hello, too.

Mrs. Jean Schmidt was short and round and gray-haired

and jolly. Marin tried to think how Mrs. Schmidt would see her family. Dad always called himself a "chrome dome" because he was mostly bald, but right now his head truly glistened because he was sweaty from all the unpacking. His University of Illinois T-shirt was soaked through, too. Beside him, Mom's "impress the new coworkers" mint-green blouse and dark slacks looked too fussy. If Mrs. Jean Schmidt had come over five minutes later, Mom would have been in a T-shirt and gym shorts, just like Dad and Marin.

Marin smoothed back the strands of hair that had come loose from her dark ponytail. A gnarled twig and a tiny leaf came off in her hand—evidently they'd been stuck in her hair ever since she'd run through the woods, and neither she nor Dad had noticed.

Marin heard Kenner's voice once again in her head: *You should pay more attention to what you look like! What if you have food stuck in your teeth, and you don't even know? That's what mirrors are for!*

The day Kenner had said that, Marin had wanted to yell back, *I thought that's what* friends *are for! If I had food stuck in my teeth, wouldn't you tell me? Nicely, I mean, not just to make fun of me . . . Isn't that what a* true *friend would do?* But the words had caught in Marin's throat.

Now she watched Mom and Dad and Mrs. Jean Schmidt talking so easily, even though they'd just met. Mom and Dad were promising to let Mrs. Jean Schmidt hold baby Owen sometime when he was awake; Mrs. Jean Schmidt was telling about how she'd grown up in the very house she'd lived in now, and how her husband had died five years ago, but she hadn't had time to get lonely because her three grandsons had moved in right after that, when the oldest was just in kindergarten, and . . .

And if Mrs. Jean Schmidt lived in her house since she was a little girl, wouldn't she know about the houses on the other side of the woods? Marin wondered. *Wouldn't she know about those teenagers?*

"What . . . ?" Marin began, and all three of the grown-ups looked at her.

And what was she supposed to say after that? *What do you know about kids in the neighborhood who can disappear from one place and magically reappear somewhere else?* If she asked that, Mrs. Jean Schmidt would think she was crazy. Mom and Dad would think she was just making up a story. She couldn't tell them about this any more than she'd been able to tell anyone about what had happened with Kenner and Ashlyn.

Marin gulped.

"What are your grandsons' names?" she asked, and didn't even bother listening for the answer.

SIX

Marin went back to the woods the next afternoon.

"Maybe we could invite Mrs. Jean Schmidt's grandsons over, if you want someone to play with," Dad had suggested as Marin reached for the handle of the sliding glass door to go outside. "We could return the favor of her bringing us dinner last night, maybe give her some peace and quiet for a while. . . ."

"What if *I* want peace and quiet, after unpacking all these boxes?" Marin had snapped, in a way that made Dad take a step back.

For a moment, Dad just looked at her. Then he murmured, "I keep forgetting—you *are* eleven, and you've been working hard, and you should get to choose how you spend your free time."

There was nothing of jokey, laughing gym-teacher Dad in his voice, and he looked so sad all of sudden that Marin almost whirled around and said, *No, no, we'll do whatever you want! You can choose for me!*

But she couldn't stop thinking about the teenagers in the house on the other side of the woods. She slipped outside, leaving Dad behind with baby Owen and the still-substantial wall of boxes.

It was another sunny June day, but once again the light became dim and murky after Marin took three or four steps into the woods. She tiptoed this time rather than running, because she was pretty sure that baby Owen had slept longer after lunch than he did yesterday, and so the mysterious teenagers might already be home from school. Or, for all Marin knew, yesterday might have been their last day of school for the year, and they'd been home all day.

But they were doing homework yesterday—who does homework on the last day of school?

Maybe high school kids did. Or maybe just high school kids did who were also capable of disappearing and reappearing at will.

Marin didn't know enough about anything.

That sounds like something Kenner would say about me, Marin thought.

She didn't want to be thinking about Kenner out in these woods, where little purple flowers spread like a carpet before her, and people who looked like sunbeams lay ahead of her. She wanted to believe that Pennsylvania was going to be totally different from Illinois, and she'd left everything bad behind her.

Mrs. Jean Schmidt seems happy here, Marin thought, and giggled. Mrs. Jean Schmidt seemed like the type of person who would be happy anywhere.

And just like that, Marin's mood turned. She felt brave and intrepid, marching off into the woods by herself, climbing higher and higher up the hill, going back toward the scene that had frightened her only yesterday.

When she got to the tree she'd scrambled up the day before, she peeked around the trunk first. Too many bushes and leafy branches blocked her view of the teenagers' house and yard at ground level. She had to go higher.

This time she got a toehold into a knothole on the trunk, so she didn't have to scrape her legs by flipping around as she climbed onto the lowest branch. After that everything was easy, as if the tree had purposely grown its branches like a winding staircase. But Marin ascended slowly, pausing after every step to gaze out. She didn't want to shake the branches any more than a squirrel or a chipmunk would, and make anyone who might be watching suspicious. She also wanted to be like a detective, gathering clues anywhere she could.

On the second branch up, she was at eye level with two windows at the side of the teenagers' house. But gauzy curtains covered the windows, making everything behind them indistinct. Was a figure moving inside one of the rooms, or had a breeze just ruffled the curtains? It was hard to tell when so much inside the house was hidden in shadow, and Marin had to shade her eyes from the bright sun overhead to peer in.

She climbed higher, and both the front and backyard of the house came into view.

Both were empty.

Did the teenagers follow the same routine every day? Was she too late for homework time on the back patio?

Where did the teenagers go after that?

Marin studied the teenagers' patio, with its empty wooden picnic table and empty wicker lounge chairs with the gaudy orange-and-green cushions. A pencil lay nestled between two of the slats of the picnic table, but there was no other evidence of the homework session from the day before. Or from any activity that might have taken place there today. Marin shifted her focus to the pots of flowers that lined both the patio and the front porch, overflowing with pink-and-white petunias and purple-and-yellow pansies. The colors blurred together. But something—a stick? a miniature flag?—nestled in the blossoms and leaves of the flowerpot closest to Marin's tree. If the object was a flag, it wasn't a red, white, and blue one; it blended in too well with the blooms around it. Had that been there before?

Was it some kind of new clue?

The woods around her seemed extra quiet and extra still all of a sudden, as if even the trees were waiting to see what she would do.

Dad wouldn't want me trespassing in someone else's yard, but if I could just find a gap in the bushes down below, I could peek out and see that flag better. And maybe see into the house better, and see if anyone really is home . . .

The bushes directly below Marin's tree were like a solid wall. But off to the side, in an area that faced a deeper portion of the teenagers' backyard, there was a section where the bushes looked a little sickly. They weren't as tall as the others around them, and either some of their branches were only dead wood, or they hadn't grown leaves yet after the winter.

Marin began shinnying down, aiming for that spot.

When she got to the ground, she stopped and listened. Nothing. She crept through the underbrush, keeping an image in her mind of the view from overhead. The shorter bushes were farther away than she'd thought, and she had to skirt around brambles to get there. But finally she stood at the edge of the teenagers' yard, with a clear view of the back of their house.

And now she was too far away from the flowerpot to see the flag planted in its dirt. Maybe the flag wasn't even tall enough to stick out over the edge of the flowerpot; maybe the only way to see it was from above, or from right beside it.

But that flowerpot was so close to the bushes . . . Maybe if Marin just walked just along the yard-side of the bushes, she could see the flag.

And it wouldn't be like trespassing, because I'd still be mostly in the woods. . . .

Marin glanced once more toward the house. From this angle, she could tell there were no lights on inside. No one was home.

Marin squeezed between leafless branches, inching toward the teenagers' yard.

"Stop!" someone suddenly cried above her.

SEVEN

Marin looked up. She saw a shoe balanced on a tree branch high overhead, and then, beside it, a hand pointing toward the teenagers' house and yard.

She whipped her head around. The French doors that led from the teenagers' house to the patio had just swung open, but nobody stood in the doorway; nobody clutched the doorknob.

It was like the door had opened all by itself.

"But what . . . where . . . ," she gasped. She peered back up toward the tree. "What's going on?"

"Get away from here! Run!"

It was the voice from above again, but she couldn't see the shoe or the hand anymore. And the voice seemed to be coming from a different tree—had whoever it belonged to jumped?

A tree shook a few yards away, as if someone was frantically scrambling down through its branches. Rather than running, Marin took a step toward that tree.

"Wait—who are you? Are we in danger?" Marin called. She kept her voice soft, partly out of fear of being overheard, partly because her vocal cords felt a little paralyzed.

She dared to glance back at the house with its open door, which was now swinging shut. Her vision seemed to sway in and out of focus. She heard a thud behind her: the tree climber had jumped down and hit the ground.

"Wait . . . ," she called again.

But whoever was behind the shoe and the hand and the thud wasn't waiting. Branches shook, and vines whipped back and forth. After staring off into the brightness of the teenagers' open backyard, Marin's eyes couldn't adjust quickly enough to the dimness of the woods. She caught a glimpse of brown hair streaming out behind someone's fleeing head, and then a particularly leafy vine swung back toward her, blocking her view.

"What are you running *from*?" Marin asked, scrambling toward the swaying vine and the thudding of running feet.

Blindly she chased after whoever was running ahead of her, but she couldn't catch up. A particularly thorny branch snagged her shirt, and she had to stop and yank it away. And then she listened. . . . The sound of running was dimmer and farther away than ever; she couldn't be sure if she was hearing actual footsteps or just the echo of footsteps.

When we get to the open part of our backyard, it'll be easier to see, she thought.

She took off running again, trying to make up the distance. She couldn't run full out and listen at the same time; all she could hear was the pounding of her own footsteps, the rasp of her own breathing.

And then she burst out of the woods, and everything was wrong.

Instead of the sunshine-yellow paint of her own family's house before her, she saw faded brown siding on a building that seemed to have had several extra rooms added on: a screened-in porch on one side, a second-story level that jutted out oddly on the other.

She wasn't in her own backyard anymore. She didn't have any idea where she was.

EIGHT

Marin felt a wave of panic. *Why did I chase the runner? I should have taken the same path out of the woods I took into it. Or left breadcrumbs, like Hansel and Gretel . . .*

Then she heard Dad's booming voice.

"There you are, pumpkin!" he said. "You found my note!"

"Note?" Marin repeated stupidly as she whirled around.

And there was Dad, standing beside Mrs. Jean Schmidt and an ancient metal swing set in a little clearing right at the edge of the woods. It looked like Dad had just finished placing baby Owen into Mrs. Jean Schmidt's arms—he was still moving his arms back. Beyond them, little kids swarmed over the swing set. Marin blinked and gazed all around.

The strange brown building before her must be the back of Mrs. Jean Schmidt's house. Marin let her gaze wander downhill, past the house's sagging sun porch and a little rock ledge. Off to the side, she saw lilac and forsythia—the bushes that grew beside her own patio. Their branches had blocked her view of Mrs. Jean Schmidt's yard and house when she'd been in her own yard.

Dad pointed toward their house and then back into the woods, as if he was trying to figure things out, too.

"Oh, so you didn't see my note, but you knew to run over this way anyhow?" he asked. He turned briefly back to Mrs. Jean Schmidt. "See? Wasn't I telling you that *both* my kids are amazing? Even I didn't realize that Marin is telepathic!"

Mrs. Jean Schmidt laughed, but Marin didn't.

"No, I was just . . . ," she began. Dad's joke made it hard to hold on to the feeling of a moment ago, when she'd been running so frantically through the woods. And she wanted to hold on to that—she wanted to understand what she'd seen. "I didn't know that I *wouldn't* end up back at our house. Isn't there a fence or something between the yards?"

Mrs. Jean Schmidt laughed again.

"Who'd want to bother maintaining a fence back in those woods? Wilderness like that, it takes over anything humans try to build. Believe me, honey, you're welcome to wander over into my section of the woods any time you want." She patted the blanket wrapped around baby Owen and peered down into his face. "And you, little man, when you grow up a little, you're welcome, too. This is a friendly neighborhood. Always has been. Always will be."

Then why did someone yell, "Stop!" at me? Marin

wondered. *Why did whoever it was yell, "Get away from here!" and "Run!" when I started asking questions?*

Maybe it'd been a long time since Mrs. Jean Schmidt had stepped foot into the woods. What did she know anymore about what was back there?

Maybe not in the woods, but . . .

Marin darted her glance toward the gap between Mrs. Jean Schmidt's house and the stone wall.

"Did you see someone run out of the woods ahead of me?" she asked. She thought about the size of the shoe and the hand she'd seen; she thought about how she hadn't needed to tilt her head upward to see the runner's brown hair streaming out behind his or her head. "Another kid, maybe? Someone about my age?"

Dad and Mrs. Jean Schmidt both shook their heads. But then Mrs. Jean Schmidt added, "Oh, did you see another kid in the woods? That was probably my grandson. The oldest. Charley. He roams around back there a lot."

Marin looked more closely at the little kids on the swing set, a girl with a headful of braids and two boys in matching overalls. Preschoolers.

"Didn't you say your oldest grandson was just in kindergarten?" Marin asked. Did Mrs. Jean Schmidt let a kindergartener roam around in the woods by himself?

And how could a kindergartener be as tall as Marin?

"No, I said he was in kindergarten when he came to live with me," Mrs. Jean Schmidt corrected. "He's ten now, almost eleven, and the twins are eight. Fifth and third graders. I mean, that's what they *were*. Today was their last day."

So elementary school's out now, Marin thought. *Would school have ended for those teenagers, too?*

Was there a way to ask that question? Marin's head swam a little, still trying to sort everyone out. If Mrs. Schmidt's grandsons were in third and fifth grade, then she didn't have a clue who these little kids were on the swing set.

"Oh—these three aren't mine," Mrs. Schmidt said, her gaze following Marin's. "I babysit sometimes."

"My mommy said she would turn into a monster if she didn't go to yoga today," the little girl said solemnly.

"We can't have that happening!" Mrs. Schmidt laughed. "And this way, I get to have fun with the three of you wee ones. And you get to meet our new neighbors, Marin and baby Owen and"—she turned to Marin's dad—"is it okay if I tell the kids to call you Mr. Kevin?"

"Fine by me," Dad said.

Mrs. Jean Schmidt began explaining the names and ages of each of the preschoolers, and possibly their entire life histories as well. How could Marin switch the conversation back to the boy in the woods?

She got lucky: Dad did it for her.

"You know, Marin just finished fifth grade," he said when Mrs. Jean Schmidt took a breath. "So I guess she and your grandson will be at the middle school together in the fall. It'll be nice for her to know someone else, starting out."

"Oh, Charley won't be going to the middle school," Mrs. Jean Schmidt said. She wasn't looking at Marin or Dad now. She kept her head bent low over baby Owen, as if it took all her concentration to pat his cheek. "Charley has his own school. It's a little bit . . . different."

Dad's expression stayed cheerful and friendly.

"Well, then Charley and Marin can just be neighborhood friends," he said with a shrug. "It's good to have friends lots of different places."

Mrs. Jean Schmidt switched to focusing on patting the tuft of hair at the top of Owen's head.

"Sure," she said. "That would be great. If Charley ever comes out of the woods!"

She laughed, and that should have been enough to turn her words into a joke.

But it wasn't.

NINE

"What do you think Mrs. Schmidt meant when she said her grandson's school was different?" Marin asked Dad as soon as they stepped back into their own house.

Dad pulled the sliding glass door shut behind them.

"I think," he said, "she meant it wasn't like Summitview Middle."

Marin kicked off her shoes and left them by the door.

"But how?" she asked. "Did she mean—"

"I think if she'd wanted us to know more than that, she would have used another word instead," Dad said.

"But—"

"Marin," Dad said warningly, in the same tone he used with kids who argued that they'd been safe on base when he called them out, or kids who claimed someone else had cheated, when really they themselves weren't following the rules.

Or kids who said they didn't want to be on the same team as the kid who couldn't run very well.

"I'm not being rude!" Marin protested. "I don't want to call him names or be mean to him if he has autism or special needs or whatever. I'm just asking because—"

"You want to know a label?" Dad said quietly.

"No!" Marin exploded. "I want to know why he ran away when I saw him in the woods! I want to know how Mrs. Schmidt could say this was always a friendly neighborhood, when her own grandson wasn't friendly!"

It was safe to say that much, wasn't it? Marin bit her lip, so she didn't go on and say, *And how could those teenagers I saw just disappear? How could a door open on its own? What if Charley made me miss my chance to find an explanation?*

In an instant, Dad had his arm around Marin's shoulders. He shifted to holding Owen in only one arm so he could engulf her in a bear hug.

"Oh, Marin, I know," he said. "I should have seen that. Moving is hard, isn't it? For all we know, maybe this Charley kid isn't really capable of being friendly, because of some issue that's outside his control. That wouldn't be his fault, or yours. And it's not really any of our business." For a minute, Marin thought he was going into the usual lecture he gave kids at school about being kind to everyone, no matter what. But he didn't. "I promise, in no time at all, you'll have friends here, too, just like you did back in Illinois. Friends like Kenner and Ashlyn."

Marin sniffled, and she figured Dad would think it was because she missed Kenner and Ashlyn. He went on, "Would it help to FaceTime or Skype with them? We can do that, you know. You don't just have to stick to texting or—"

"That wouldn't help," Marin mumbled into Dad's T-shirt. "That would . . . make things worse."

She didn't have to tell him why.

She didn't have to tell him that she hadn't texted either Ashlyn or Kenner once since she'd left Illinois.

They hadn't texted her, either.

Owen whimpered, as if Marin was upsetting him, too. Or maybe he was just protesting being smooshed between Dad and Marin.

Marin pulled back.

"The way Mrs. Jean Schmidt made it sound, I'll probably never see this Charley kid again," she said. "She acted surprised that I saw him at all."

"It's like he's the Bigfoot of Summitview forest," Dad agreed. "Or Paul Bunyan. Was he eight feet tall? Was he wandering around with a blue ox named Babe? Charley Schmidt—the boy, the myth, the legend! And, believe it or not, Marin Pluckett actually saw him, even though he was running faster than the breeze! *She* must have superpower vision!"

Dad lifted Owen high in the air, as if he was pretending to

be Paul Bunyan, and the baby's weight was no more than a feather to him. Owen's whimper turned into a gurgle of joy.

"Oh, you like that?" Dad asked, lowering Owen again and peering down into the baby's face, as if Owen could answer. "I'd totally forgotten until now—Marin, I used to do this with you all the time when you were a baby."

Now Dad began acting more like he was a weight lifter, and Owen was the barbell. Owen cooed happily.

"This always stopped you from crying, too," Dad told Marin as he lifted Owen up, then down again. "Why didn't I remember this move sooner? We needed this last night at two a.m.!"

He began dancing around, swinging Owen up and down and side to side, as if the two of them had an entire workout routine planned.

"I'm the baby whisperer!" Dad bragged. "And I'll be in the best shape of my life for all the job interviews I'm going to have this summer!"

It was impossible to avoid laughing at Dad when he got like this.

"Marin! Get the iPad! We need music! And join us!" he shouted.

Marin obediently turned on the same warm-up music Dad used for his gym classes. He grabbed her hand, and alternated twirling her and raising and lowering baby Owen.

"You're trying to distract me!" she accused when he spun her close.

"Is it working?" Dad asked, waggling his eyebrows at her.

Marin rolled her eyes and nodded. But that really wasn't true. She was still thinking about Charley Schmidt.

Next time I find him in the woods, she told herself, *I'll get him to tell me everything about the teenagers.*

Marin had seen nothing of Charley Schmidt but his hand and his shoe in the tree, and the one quick glimpse of his hair, streaming out behind him as he ran away.

But surely he knew the teenagers' secret.

He had to.

TEN

The next day was Saturday, and Mom was home. And it was such a beautiful sunny day that Dad rebelled against unpacking any more boxes and insisted that the whole family go for a long hike instead.

"You're being nice to me, aren't you?" Mom asked. "Trying to give me an actual day off . . . Really, I *can* help with the unpacking."

Dad held up his right hand like he was making a solemn vow.

"No, no, I swear, I am being totally selfish," he said. "And selfish on Marin's behalf, too. We can't face any more boxes. I don't care if we're still unpacking boxes next February—who cares if we're stuck indoors in February, when it's going to be horrible outside anyway? We just can't stay inside today. It would be wrong."

They packed a lunch and hiked for hours. And it was a perfect day. Even Owen barely cried. Except for when he was eating, he slept the whole time in the carrier Dad strapped to his chest.

"This is our life now," Mom marveled as they reached the crest of a hill. "We have a new baby. We're a family of four. We live in Pennsylvania."

"You're the *dean* of your college," Dad said.

"More importantly, Owen actually let us sleep four hours straight last night," Mom said. "I actually feel human again!"

Dad stepped out onto a rock at the top of the hill and shouted down toward the valley below, "Hello, Pennsylvania! We're the In Family!"

He grinned at Marin. She was the one who had suggested Owen's name, and how it would fit with not just her name, but her parents', too. Their first names were Ellen and Kevin. So all four of them were *in*. When Mom and Dad agreed with her idea, Marin had felt so proud.

Later, after everything that happened with Kenner and Ashlyn, Marin thought maybe Mom and Dad should have stuck with their original plan to name Owen "Oliver." So he wouldn't be like her.

Mom joined Dad on the rock.

"We're *in* love!" she yelled, threading her arm around Dad's waist.

"And *in*spired!" Dad added, hugging her back.

"And only somewhat *in*sane!" Mom again.

Dad motioned for Marin to join them on the rock. Marin stepped up.

"Your turn," Mom said, draping her free arm around Marin's shoulders.

Marin stared out at the valley that spread before them. This was the other side of the mountain from where they lived, the side that was mostly a national forest. It was like standing on the edge of a sea of green. Or maybe a carpet of emeralds. She could imagine someone with magical powers striding across the treetops, bouncing from one to another.

Maybe the mysterious teenagers who lived behind her had that power, too.

"Yell whatever you want," Dad urged.

Marin opened her mouth.

"Uh, hi?" she said in a normal voice.

It sounded so lame and pitiful after Mom's and Dad's shouting. Their voices had seemed to echo and magnify, filling the sky and the valley below. Marin's came out more like a pebble dropped by mistake. Embarrassing.

"I don't really want to shout anything," she said. "Standing here makes me feel more like whispering. Or just being quiet."

"That's fine," Mom said. "We can all try that."

"Even I can stop talking every now and—" Dad began, ending abruptly when Mom clapped her hand over his mouth.

The three of them stood in silence for a long moment. Mom kept her arm around Marin's shoulders; Dad held one arm around Mom's waist and one around Owen's back. It was so quiet Marin could hear Owen's sleep breathing. Down below, birds chirped in the trees, and a gentle breeze sighed through the leaves.

Then the silence started feeling wrong, as if it wasn't natural for Mom and Dad not to talk. As if Marin had forced them to act different than they really were.

"You can go back to shouting now," Marin said.

"I think we need to go back, period," Mom said, glancing at her Fitbit. "Get home before my muscles remember that I sat all week, and they weren't really prepared for this. And before it gets dark, and we can't see the trail."

"You think it's going to be dark before we get home?" Marin asked.

"I'm allowing for the possibility that I might have to crawl the last mile or so," Mom said with a mocking grin. Then she tilted her head thoughtfully. "And, you know, we could stop for dinner on the drive back . . ."

"Yes!" Dad cried, pumping a fist in the air. "We successfully avoided unpacking any boxes today!"

Even after the long hike, even with Owen strapped to his chest, he still managed a victory dance on top of the rock.

But all Marin could think was, *And I missed out on the chance to find Charley Schmidt in the woods. Or to see what the mysterious teenagers do on a Saturday . . .*

She'd just have to try on Sunday.

ELEVEN

When Marin went downstairs the next morning, Mom was pacing the living room, jostling Owen up and down. Owen was screaming, and Mom was pleading, "Please, little one, little O, please go back to sleep. Don't you want to sleep? *I* want to sleep." Then she turned and saw Marin. "Oh no—did the crying wake you? Owen had a terrible night. We probably let him sleep too much yesterday when we were hiking. Dad just went back to bed—I don't think either of us slept more than five minutes at a time."

"I didn't hear anything," Marin said. "Until now."

The first night after Mom and Dad had brought Owen home from the hospital, Marin had awakened at 3:00 a.m. to hear Owen's thin, wavery newborn cry, and Mom and Dad giggling in his room, "We forgot about this part of it, didn't we?" "Shh! You're going to wake Marin!"

But when Marin got up and poked her head in Owen's room, Mom had said, "Oh, honey, go back to bed. Get some sleep for us! Somebody in this house should be well-rested!"

After that, Owen's crying never woke Marin at night. In the morning sometimes, Mom or Dad told her, "He cried for hours!" or "I thought he was asleep again, and I was carrying him past your room and *that's* when he suddenly decided to scream—are you *sure* you didn't even hear that?"

And Marin hadn't. She was glad that she didn't have dark circles under her eyes, like Mom and Dad did. But it made her feel a little weird that something happened in her family every night that she was entirely left out of. That she didn't even know about, unless Mom and Dad told her.

Kind of like how there's something going on in the neighborhood that I don't understand. And I probably won't ever understand, unless I get Charley Schmidt to tell me. . . .

Mom kept bouncing Owen.

"So Dad and I agreed, we're still going to try to go to church this morning," Mom said. "I think we'll all feel more like we belong here once we find a church home. And you can start making friends so you'll already know other kids when school starts."

Marin's stomach churned at the thought of making new friends.

"That's okay," Marin said. "If you and Dad are too tired and just want to sleep—"

"No, no," Mom said. "I *need* church this morning. We're going."

An hour later, the whole family piled into the minivan they'd bought after Owen was born. Dad's polo shirt was wrinkled. Mom's hair stuck out in the back because, after calming Owen down, she hadn't had time to shower. Marin wore a red sundress from last summer that was a little tight under the arms. She hadn't known it would be like that, because she hadn't worn it since last August. And she hadn't been able to find any other summer dresses; they were probably still in one of the living room boxes.

Only Owen was at his best. He slept peacefully in his car seat, looking angelic in a little blue-striped shirt that came with its own bow tie.

"Is it wrong to suspect your own son of being possessed by demons?" Dad asked as he clicked the car seat into its base. "I swear, last night in the middle of the night I thought we were seconds away from a spewing-pea-soup-all-over-the-place scene. And look at him now. Do you think he's got his days and nights mixed up just to spite us?"

"He's not even three months old," Mom said wearily. "This is what babies do."

"Yeah, and I've aged three hundred years since he was born," Dad said. "I'm too old for this." He slid into the driver's seat and peered at Marin in the rearview mirror.

"Marin, you were so much luckier than Owen. You got us when we were young and fresh. We could stay up all night back then, no problem."

"We survived this phase with Marin. We'll survive it with Owen," Mom said. She seemed to be trying to smile as she turned around. "So, Marin, we're going to that church we passed yesterday in downtown Summitview, the one where you said the stained glass looked pretty. I checked out their website last night while I was nursing Owen, and it sounded great. Especially the programs they have for kids. But if we don't like it, we'll try a different one next week."

Marin nodded because what else could she do?

When they got to the church, an old man standing by the front door insisted on showing them around.

"If you want to keep your baby with you in the sanctuary but he starts getting fussy, we have a crying room at the back," the man said. "We have speakers in there so you can still hear the service, but you don't have to worry that you're disturbing anyone. It's soundproof."

"What a great idea!" Dad said. "We need that in our house!"

Or in schools, Marin thought. What if last school year, when Kenner and Ashlyn started being so mean to her, Marin could have just walked away? What if there'd been someplace else for her to go, away from everyone?

She tried to picture what a school crying room would be

like: There'd be lots of Kleenex boxes, of course, so crying kids wouldn't have snot and tears running down their faces. Maybe there'd be blankets where they could burrow in and hide. And maybe books, too, so they could read and think about other kids' stories, instead of their own problems.

She was making a school crying room sound like the school library. Maybe she should have spent all last spring hanging out in the library, instead of with Kenner and Ashlyn. She would have been happier that way.

Marin was thinking about this so hard that she almost missed the rest of the old man's explanations.

". . . and then your daughter can go to Sunday school after the children's message. . . . There'll be lots of other kids for her to meet. . . ."

Marin wanted to turn around and run back to the car. Or maybe just head for the crying room. All last spring, when everything was going wrong with Ashlyn and Kenner, Marin had thought, *We're moving. It'll be summer. I won't have to see any other kids over the summer. And then in the fall I'll start over at a new school, and I'll be older then, and I'll know how to make new friends. Ashlyn and Kenner won't be there. Everything will be fine.*

It was only June. She wasn't ready for new friends yet. She wasn't ready for being the new kid, and still didn't know how to make other kids like her.

What if I'm never ready? What if everything with Kenner and Ashlyn ruined me forever?

Marin shoved those thoughts out of her brain as hard as she could. She was in a church; she started praying.

Please, God. Please, please, please don't let me start crying here in front of everyone. . . .

She and Mom and Dad and Owen sat down. Owen kept sleeping, but Mom and Dad started talking to the people around them: "Haven't even been here a full week yet . . ." "Oh, yes, this part of Pennsylvania is so beautiful. . . . We're loving it." "Our kids' ages? Owen is nine weeks old today, and Marin just turned eleven. . . ."

Marin pretended to be really, really interested in reading the church bulletin.

The sanctuary filled in. The service started. After announcements and a few hymns, a woman stood up and began reading a Bible passage, one about Jesus being tempted in the desert.

So I'm going to hear about even Jesus messing up? Marin thought.

But Jesus hadn't messed up. He'd been able to resist the temptation. Because he was Jesus.

Now it was time for the children's message. Kids began streaming out of the pews; it was like a river of kids flowing down the aisles toward the front of the church. Marin saw three girls giggling together, like she and Ashlyn and Kenner used to. They all wore striped sundresses, as if they'd texted each other the night before to coordinate their outfits. Maybe they'd even bought the dresses together.

I can't try to be those girls' friends, Marin thought. *I can't. Why would they want me to be their friend?*

Marin didn't think she could even bear to walk up to the front of the church right now.

She turned to Mom to say, *You know what? I really want to hear the sermon. So I'll just stay with you and Dad.* But Mom was already giving Marin's shoulder a little nudge. Mom's face was glowing, expectant—overjoyed that Marin would get a chance to meet other kids.

There was nothing Marin could say to convince Mom and Dad to let her skip Sunday school.

Then a miracle happened: Owen started crying.

"Here," Marin whispered, scooping her baby brother out of Mom's arms. "I'll take him to the crying room so you and Dad can stay for church."

Mom pulled back a little.

"No, no, it's not fair to you—" she began.

But one of the women Mom and Dad had been talking to earlier turned around and whispered, "Your daughter's being kind to you. Let her do that!"

And Mom let Marin take Owen.

Marin hurried down the aisle toward the crying room,

away from the kids gathering on the steps at the front of the church. Owen's wails echoed behind her as she carried him out. But Marin didn't mind the adults staring at her along the aisles. They mostly looked sympathetic, as if they'd had to carry crying babies out of the church themselves. She heard one woman whisper, "What a sweet big sister!"

Marin nestled her chin against Owen's head. He felt different in her arms now than he ever had before. It was almost like they were partners, working together. It was almost as though he'd understood what she'd needed. She lifted him a little higher, so his ear was right beside her mouth.

"You are the best baby brother ever," she whispered.

TWELVE

That afternoon, Mom and Dad slept while Owen napped.

"Sorry your parents are so boring," Mom apologized as she tiptoed out of Owen's room. "We just . . ." Whatever else she'd planned to say was swallowed up in a giant yawn.

"That's okay," Marin said. "I'm going to play in the backyard."

But when she went to slide open the back door, she saw that it had started raining. And it was the kind of rain that lashed down through the trees, driven by a fierce wind.

Even if Marin braved the downpour, there was no way the mysterious teenagers would be hanging around outside their house today, where Marin could watch them. There was no way even Charley Schmidt would be wandering the woods today, for Marin to find him.

If Marin were more like Mom and Dad, she would have marched over to Mrs. Jean Schmidt's house—even in the rain—and knocked on the door and asked, "Can I meet your grandson now?"

But Marin wasn't like Mom and Dad.

She started to read a book, but she kept looking up every other sentence to see if the rain had stopped yet, so she couldn't enjoy it. She switched to turning on the TV really, really low so she wouldn't wake the rest of her family. But she couldn't find anything she wanted to watch. She pulled out the iPad that had been a whole-family gift last Christmas, and thought about playing a game.

Then she thought of something better to do with the iPad. She typed in the word *invisibility* and hit enter.

Wikipedia told her that invisibility meant that an object couldn't be seen.

Oh, thanks, Wikipedia, she thought.

Farther down, there were links about scientists being close to inventing invisibility cloaks, like in Harry Potter. But when she clicked on the articles, they were about carbon nanotubes and metamaterials and other things she didn't understand.

Anyhow, if the teenagers she'd seen—and then, *not* seen— had had invisibility cloaks, wouldn't she have seen them putting on the cloaks?

She pushed the iPad aside and began making a list on a piece of paper: *Who Can Become Invisible?*

Superheroes

Ghosts

Mutants

Aliens

All of those seemed wrong. In stories, superheroes and mutants were always fighting some enemy. Aliens did, too— they usually wanted to conquer the Earth. And ghosts tried to scare people to get revenge, or to keep a treasure hidden, or something like that. The teenagers Marin had seen hadn't been fighting, or practicing to fight. They hadn't seemed scary. They'd just seemed like regular teenagers. Except for being able to disappear.

Angels, she thought. *Demons?*

Those didn't seem right, either. Marin crumpled up the paper and looked out the sliding glass door again.

It had stopped raining.

Finally! she thought.

Just then she heard Owen begin to cry.

Oh no! Now Mom and Dad will wake up; now they'll be all, "Oh, Marin, we're so sorry we've been ignoring you. We promise, we'll spend the rest of the afternoon with you. Want to play a game?"

Marin couldn't let a whole other day pass without figuring out anything else about the teenagers on the other side of the woods. Quickly she raced up the stairs and into Owen's room. He hadn't abandoned himself completely to wailing yet; when he saw her, he stopped crying for a moment. His lower lip quivered; his fists waved helplessly in the air.

"Shh, shh," Marin whispered. "Help me out again, little O."

Owen screwed up his face like he was preparing to scream.

"Maybe you want to come out to the woods with me?" Marin suggested.

She scooped him into her arms. Maybe it was just the surprise that kept Owen from crying again. Maybe he understood somehow that she needed his help. But he didn't make another peep as she whisked him down the stairs.

In the kitchen she paused to grab a bottle for Owen, and to slide him and the bottle into the same baby carrier that Dad had used yesterday in the state park. Then she wrote two notes, one to leave on the kitchen counter, and one to leave in Owen's crib. Both said the same thing:

Owen woke up and started crying. I took him to the backyard so he wouldn't wake you two up. Don't worry—I took a bottle to feed him with, too. And his diaper isn't dirty. We won't be gone long.

That covered everything, didn't it?

Snuggled against Marin, Owen lost the worried look of being on the verge of tears. He even giggled a little as Marin dashed upstairs to put the note in his crib. Then, quickly, she raced down the stairs again and out the sliding door.

It was cooler outside now, after the rain. Marin's sneakers slid on the wet grass, so she had to step carefully until she reached the pebbled path into the woods.

"Don't worry, Owen," she murmured. "You know I wouldn't drop you. Even if I fell, even if the carrier straps broke, I'd hold on."

He gazed steadily at her face, his expression entirely calm now, his dark eyes glowing. It was like just looking at her made him happy. Owen had only known her for nine weeks—he only had nine weeks of experience knowing *anyone*—and yet he trusted her completely.

He thought she was a good person.

Somehow that made her feel ashamed.

"Thanks for the help this morning, little dude," she said, patting his back. "It's not really that I'm scared of other kids. Not usually. It's just . . . just . . ."

Owen was only nine weeks old. He was completely innocent. He didn't know anything about how mean kids could be sometimes. Did Marin really want to be the one who told him?

"Anyway, those moms in the crying room were nice, didn't you think?" Marin said instead.

She thought about the way the three women she'd found sitting in the crying room had oohed and aahed over Owen, and insisted that Marin take one of the rocking chairs. They'd introduced themselves and their babies—one of the babies had been named Oliver, even, so Marin had been able to say that that had been the backup-choice name for Owen.

But there'd also been a moment when one of the women had pointed at the other two and said, "Yeah, Heather and Lisa have known each other since preschool, but my family's pretty new to Summitview, too. We've only been here two years." And she'd sounded so wistful.

It was funny how they'd used their first names to Marin, as though Marin taking care of Owen made her seem older than eleven.

Or maybe moving and taking care of Owen had made Marin *become* more mature, so she could notice an adult woman sounding wistful like that.

It was like that woman was telling Marin that Heather and Lisa made that woman feel as left out as Kenner and Ashlyn made Marin feel toward the end, back in Illinois.

Could *adults* have problems making friends, too? After two years, even?

"But Ashlyn and me, *we* were the ones who'd been friends since we were really little," Marin told Owen now. "We didn't even meet Kenner until fourth grade. And the three of us were fine, all through fourth grade. It wasn't until fifth grade that Kenner started being mean. And then Ashlyn was, too. And then . . ."

Owen just kept staring up at her. Listening.

"Someday, you're going to be able to understand everything you hear, and I won't be able to talk to you like this," Marin said. "I'll have to be careful about what I say to you, just like I am with Mom and Dad."

Marin's voice sounded too loud in the quiet woods. Maybe the rain had sent all the birds and squirrels and chipmunks and other animals into hiding, because she couldn't hear a single peep or squawk or chirrup. It felt like Marin and Owen had the woods entirely to themselves.

Marin stopped talking and started tiptoeing. Maybe if she was as quiet as the birds and squirrels and chipmunks and other animals, she could sneak up on Charley Schmidt, and find him before he had a chance to run away from her.

Maybe she could sneak up on the teenagers and catch them disappearing or reappearing again.

Maybe, if she was quiet enough, she could find answers to everything she wanted to know. Without even having to ask the questions.

The path she was on split, and Marin decided to follow the direction that led deeper into the woods behind the Schmidt house, rather than the trail that led directly to the teenagers' house. But this path was more rambling, circling back on itself, cresting hillocks and then dropping down into mini valleys.

She saw what looked like the largest hillock yet before her. But as she got closer, she realized it was actually a vine-covered, overgrown, half-collapsed wooden structure.

An old shed? A playhouse? She crept closer, reaching out a hand to push back some of the vines. But her foot slipped into an unexpected gully in the path, and she tripped forward, coming down hard on her right knee. She managed to keep Owen upright, wrapping her arms protectively around the back of his carrier to hug him close. But he let out a little whimper of surprise at the jolt. His eyes widened, and then he twisted up his whole face.

"No, no—please don't cry!" Marin whispered. "You're fine! Everything's okay! I'm sorry!"

She touched his cheek, and he reached out and wrapped his tiny fingers around her pinkie. His face smoothed out, and he let out a little snuffling sound of contentment.

"That's right—you hold on to me, I'll hold on to you . . ." Marin murmured.

She looked back at the half-collapsed shed, and the vine she'd been reaching for was gone, whipped to the side to reveal another kid. He was almost exactly the same height as her, with brown eyes and a skinny face, and thick brown hair that skimmed his shoulders. He wore a green T-shirt, and shorts the same gray as the weathered wood behind him. Marin wouldn't have looked twice at those clothes on anyone else, but somehow they made this kid seem like part of the forest. He could have been one of the Lost Boys in the Peter Pan story; he could have been some frontiersman wearing a coonskin cap and a deerskin coat in Marin's old social studies book back in Illinois.

But Marin was pretty sure she knew who this really was: Charley Schmidt.

"H—" Marin started to say, suddenly uncertain whether to say *Hi* or *Hello*. What was least likely to make him take off running away again?

But Charley lunged *toward* her, not away.

"You went there again, and this time you found a *baby*?" he asked breathlessly. "Is it . . . is it . . . I have to see that baby!"

And then he reached for Owen, as if he planned to yank him away from Marin.

THIRTEEN

Marin jerked away and shoved one arm out to the side to fend off Charley. With the other arm, she held on to Owen as tightly as she could.

"This is my *brother*!" she protested. "It's not just some baby I *found*. Leave him alone!"

Charley crumpled. Marin had never seen someone deflate so quickly. It hadn't quite registered how delighted he'd looked before—the grin plastered across his face, the eager gleam in his eyes, as if it was Christmas and his birthday all at once—until the grin and the gleam vanished. Now the corners of his mouth sagged like they belonged to the saddest-looking bloodhound ever; his head dropped like he no longer had energy to hold it up. He slammed against the broken doorframe of the dilapidated shed behind him as if he were broken, too.

It was like watching a helium balloon go from bobbing in the air to being flat on the ground in the blink of an eye.

"Did you lose a baby somewhere?" Marin asked, because it was impossible to keep yelling at Charley now. "Are you looking for—"

"Never mind," Charley growled. "Go away. Don't come back. And don't tell anyone I said anything."

"Who would I tell?" Marin asked.

"Grandma," Charley muttered.

Marin cradled her arm around Owen's back. She wasn't afraid of Charley now. That would be like fearing an ant crushed on the ground, like fearing a swatted fly. But it still felt like she needed to protect Owen from the grumpiness in this boy's voice.

Owen shouldn't have to hear anyone sounding so totally hopeless.

"I'm your new neighbor," Marin said. "You're Charley, right? I'm Marin. We could . . . could . . ."

She almost said, *We could be friends!*

When Charley had been about to grab her brother?

Charley picked up a stick leaning against the doorframe and began poking it into the ground, making one hole after another.

"I know who you are," he said, just as surly as before. "Grandma told me."

"Is Mrs. Jean Schmidt your grandma?" Marin asked.

Charley only shrugged, his shoulders barely moving up

and down. Marin figured he would have said no if she wasn't.

So now ask, "What do you know about other kids who live around here? Especially the ones who are older than us—the teenagers?"

Her tongue felt paralyzed. It was like she wanted to know too badly. Like she might get only one chance to ask, and she didn't want to mess it up. What if he just shrugged at that question, too?

Maybe she didn't even believe the teenagers were real. Maybe that was what kept her from asking.

Maybe she didn't want to know if they were imaginary.

Maybe she didn't want Charley thinking *she* was weird.

Charley jabbed his stick so far down into the mud that it got stuck. He grunted as he tried to jerk it back up. It still didn't budge. He gave up and glared at Marin.

"This is *my* clubhouse," he said. "Nobody else is allowed. I told you to leave."

Tears stung at Marin's eyes. Charley was the first kid her age she'd met in Pennsylvania—what if all the kids here were like this?

To Marin's horror, she felt water begin to stream down her face. She'd never just started crying like that before. Even when things got really bad with Ashlyn and Kenner, Marin had always known when she was on the verge of sobbing.

Would Charley think she was as big a baby as Owen?

Thunder cracked overhead, and Marin realized: The water on her face wasn't tears. It had started raining again.

Fat raindrops splatted against Marin's cheeks. And . . . against Owen's head.

Owen started wailing again.

Marin cupped her hands over his head, but this was the start of another torrential downpour. Marin could try running back to her house, but she and Owen would get soaked. Or she'd slip and fall on the muddy path.

That's if she could even see the path.

She'd been a terrible big sister, bringing Owen out here.

"You *have* to let me into your clubhouse until the rain stops," she snarled at Charley. "Or, at least, let Owen in." She started fumbling with the straps tying the baby carrier and Owen to her chest. "I'll watch him from out here if I have to, but . . ."

Charley's eyes widened, staring past her toward a sudden brightness behind her. A second later, thunder crackled again.

"There's lightning, and it's close—you can't stay out in this!" he cried.

And then he grabbed Marin by the arm and pulled her into the clubhouse.

FOURTEEN

The inside of the clubhouse looked totally different from the outside.

From the outside, it looked unloved and abandoned, like something from so far back in the past that nobody remembered it was there, or else someone would surely have knocked it down completely and carted away its splintered boards. From the outside, it looked like it was just a matter of time before the wilderness ate it up again, and all traces of the building disappeared entirely.

But inside . . .

Inside, the clubhouse felt like a home.

Inside, it took Marin a full minute to realize that the back side of the roof sloped down to meet up with the floor. She was too busy noticing the beanbag chairs lining the walls, the old broom leaning against the side of a window frame (Charley even *cleaned* his clubhouse?), and the solid table that stood in the center of the room—in the one spot where no water dripped through the broken roof. Colored pencils and a whole sheaf of papers lay scattered across the table.

"You like to draw?" Marin asked, moving toward the table.

"Don't look," Charley said, rushing ahead of her to stuff the papers into a drawer of the table.

"I'm just trying to go where the water won't leak on Owen," Marin said, even though that wasn't her whole reason. She really wanted to go through the sheaf of papers one by one. What would a kid like Charley draw?

"You're only allowed here until the rain stops," Charley said stiffly, as if he already regretted letting Marin and Owen in. "Will your brother ever stop crying?"

Marin hadn't even entirely noticed that Owen was still crying. She was just automatically moving side to side the same way Mom and Dad did when they were trying to soothe the baby.

"Maybe I should feed him," Marin said, pulling the bottle from its little compartment at the side of the baby carrier.

She sat down in the chair by the table and unhooked the baby carrier to lower Owen into her lap. He greedily latched onto the bottle's nipple.

Now the only sounds were the rain thudding against the roof and the occasional slurp of Owen's sucking.

Marin propped the bottle against her shoulder for a moment and felt in the back pocket of her shorts. It was empty.

"I messed up," she admitted to Charley. "I forgot to bring my phone. Mom and Dad were both taking naps, and if they wake up and see it's pouring rain and Owen and I are gone and they can't even call me to find out where I am . . . they're really going to be mad."

Charley just looked at her.

"Do *you* have a cell phone I could use to text them?" Marin asked.

"Oh!" Charley said, as if he hadn't realized that was even possible. "I forgot mine, too."

Why did it feel like he was lying?

Charley looked down at his sneakers.

"Er . . . I don't actually have a phone," he admitted. "Grandma's old-fashioned. She doesn't think kids need phones."

"Oh," Marin said. "What do your parents think?"

"Who knows?" Charley said. "I haven't seen them in five years. Not *really*."

He said it like a challenge, like he wanted Marin to say, *Oh, that's awful!* or *Why? What happened?* just so he could snarl back, *It's none of your business.* He already had a sour look on his face, like he wanted to yell at her again—like that would make him happy.

Marin wanted to say, *Look, I'm a nice person. I won't tell anyone your secrets. I won't make fun of you. I won't hurt you. I promise.*

But after everything that had happened with Ashlyn and Kenner, could she really still promise that?

Owen's tiny waving hands hit against the bottle, and he started to cough.

"Oh, sorry, Owen!" Marin cried. "Sorry! Was I giving you too much all at once?"

She pulled the bottle away and started to lift him upright against her shoulder so she'd be able to pound on his back like she'd seen Mom and Dad do. But the buckle of the baby carrier strap she'd unlatched caught on the drawer of the desk; Marin pulling up on Owen also jerked against the drawer. The drawer came spilling out, tumbling toward the ground. The papers Charley had stuffed into the drawer sprang out like an explosion, one drawing after another swirling across the cracked boards of the clubhouse floor.

And every single drawing was of the teenagers Marin had seen disappear.

FIFTEEN

"Get away from there!" Charley screamed. "Don't look!"

But Marin couldn't unsee what she'd already seen.

"You've watched those kids a *lot*," Marin said, because there were dozens of drawings of the teenagers.

Charley was a good artist. His drawing of the teenagers playing Frisbee made her feel like the Frisbee was about to come sailing toward her; a drawing of the kids scrambling out of their old car made her think she could hear its rumbling engine.

But one particular drawing held her interest the most. It was like a page in a graphic novel, drawn in panels. First, the whole group of teenagers stood in the front yard, all of them laughing, their arms slung over one another's shoulders.

Then in the next panel, the outlines of the teenagers were fuzzy, as if Charley had seen them through fog, even though the house behind them stayed distinct.

In the third panel, the teenagers had vanished, leaving nothing but the house and its flowerpots behind.

Marin couldn't help herself. She snatched up that page of drawings and held it out to Charley.

"You've seen them disappear, too," she whispered. "You saw what I saw."

It was a relief to say the word *disappear* out loud.

Charley's face trembled, and he blinked hard. It was like watching Owen's face when he was about to cry.

But Charley didn't reach out and grab the drawings from Marin. He just stood there, his face spasming.

"I didn't know what you'd seen," he finally said. "I . . . I wondered."

Marin spread the drawings across the table. It seemed like this was okay now. She wanted to get them off the floor and away from Owen's waving arms. She absentmindedly held Owen against her shoulder and patted his back as she regarded the drawings. He made gurgling sounds in her ear.

"Who *are* they?" she asked. "How can they . . ."

"I used to call them the Remarkables," Charley said. "When I first found them."

His voice came out sounding strangely bitter, even though the words sounded nice. It was like biting into a cookie and discovering it was flavored with pepper instead of chocolate.

"Remarkables?" Marin repeated. "That fits. Besides

disappearing, do they have any other . . ."

She wanted to say *magical abilities* or something like that, but the scowl on Charley's face stopped her.

"Superpowers?" he finished for her. He bit off the word like it hurt. "You're like I was when I first saw them. You think they're the good guys, right? You think they look so nice and friendly and kind? I did, too. I thought I'd discovered some superheroes' hideout, and I started planning how I'd watch them, and I'd learn how to be like them, so someday they'd ask me to be a hero with them. I'd save people from . . . well, never mind. I'd save people. I was only nine then. I was stupid."

He was breathing hard, as if he'd been running fast, instead of just talking fast.

"How can you be so sure they *aren't* superheroes?" Marin asked, because she didn't want to give that up. She wanted Charley to be wrong.

She wanted to be a kid who'd discovered superheroes.

Charley laughed, and it was a laugh that sent her back to some of the worst days in Illinois, when she'd walk into her classroom in the morning and find Ashlyn and Kenner giggling together, and she knew they were giggling at her; she knew they were making fun of her. Charley wasn't making fun of her exactly. But fifth grade had taught Marin that laughter wasn't just fun. It could also be a weapon, like a sword cutting someone down to size.

Charley's laugh was the kind that hurt.

"Because I found out who they really are," he said. "They're time travelers. From the past. And something awful is about to happen because of them."

SIXTEEN

"Oh," Marin said, which was the lamest, most inadequate response ever.

Owen let out a burp just then, which was always the cue at home for Mom and Dad to laugh and laugh. *That's my boy!* Dad would say. *You show that air who's boss!* And Mom would say, *Behold the marvels of the human body!*

It was crazy that Owen belching could make them so happy.

In this clubhouse, a second after Charley said the words *time travelers*, Owen's burp seemed to break a spell.

Charley snatched the drawing of the disappearing Remarkables from the table. He brushed past Marin and Owen and began sweeping all the pictures back into the drawer.

"Never mind," he said. "None of this has anything to do with you. Forget I said anything. Forget what you saw. It'd be better for you."

"But . . . they're my neighbors," Marin said. "They live right behind me. I can't just . . ."

"Don't you get it?" Charley asked. "They're not really there. They weren't your neighbors twenty years ago when everything happened. When you see them, all you're seeing is the past."

"You weren't here twenty years ago, either," Marin protested.

Charley's shoulder-length hair swung forward to hide his face as he leaned over the table. Marin could barely see the tip of his nose.

"But my . . . ," he began, and stopped.

Just then, Marin heard a shout from the direction of her house: "Mar-in! Where are you?"

"That's my dad," Marin said.

He wasn't whisper-yelling this time. He was full-out yelling, and he sounded worried. Maybe even mad.

Marin stepped over to the door and shoved it open. The rain had stopped while she and Charley were talking, and she hadn't even noticed. Leaves dripped with fresh raindrops, but high overhead, the sun was trying to come out.

"I'm out here, Dad!" she called. "I'll be right there!" She patted her brother's head. "And don't worry—I've still got Owen!"

Her voice wasn't as powerful as Dad's. She was pretty sure he couldn't hear her.

She turned to face Charley again.

"I've got to go," she said. "But I'll be back tomorrow. We can talk more then."

Charley stayed hunched over his drawings, his elbows and arms and hands hiding them all.

"Don't bother," he muttered. "There's nothing to talk about."

"Sure there is!" Marin said. "We—"

Charley spun around. He narrowed his eyes into slits and his mouth into a thin line, as if he was trying to make his whole face into a warning sign.

"It doesn't matter what you do," he said. "*I* won't be here tomorrow, waiting for you. I'll run away if I see you coming."

His voice was soft, his words almost gentle.

And yet this felt crueler than anything Ashlyn or Kenner had ever said to Marin.

SEVENTEEN

Dad wasn't angry.

He stood in the doorway peering out toward the backyard, and his whole face burst into a grin when Marin brushed aside the last branch of the woods and stepped out onto the grass.

"You," he crowed, "are the most considerate daughter ever. I just got the best nap I've gotten since Owen was born. Thank you, thank you, thank you. I could climb Mount Everest now. I could run a marathon. I could even understand all the paperwork we signed when we bought this house!"

"Then why were you yelling for me?" Marin asked.

She glanced back toward the woods behind her. Could she just hand Owen to Dad and run back to Charley and his clubhouse?

Would Charley even let her back in?

Probably not, she thought.

"Oh!" Dad jumped a little, as though he'd forgotten he'd been yelling. "Okay, maybe my brain synapses aren't *totally* healed from nine weeks of sleep deprivation. But they're getting there. I feel like I *have* a brain again, anyway. I have a question for you. Someone from that church we visited called while your mom and I were sleeping, and they left a message . . . their Vacation Bible School is the week after next, and they said their registration deadline was already past, but they saw you there this morning and heard we were new to Summitview, and they said they could squeeze you in. . . . Wasn't that nice of them? What do you think? Wouldn't that be more fun than unpacking boxes?"

Dad had his phone in his hand, a finger poised over the screen, as if he were all ready to call back and say, *Oh, yeah! Of course Marin wants to go to your Vacation Bible School! Thank you so much!*

Back in Illinois, up until last summer, Marin had always taken Ashlyn to VBS with her. Ashlyn hadn't gone to her same church, but after four summers of VBS, she knew all the songs as well as Marin did; she was as excited as Marin was about becoming one of the older kids and getting to tie-dye her own T-shirt in crafts, instead of just watching the crafts helpers do it.

Last summer, Marin had invited both Ashlyn and Kenner, and everything had been different. Ashlyn and Kenner wanted to stand at the back of every group activity so they could whisper together instead of participating; they laughed when Marin wanted to volunteer to be snack helper. And during music, Kenner complained that the songs were stupid.

"You're right! I hate them, too!" Ashlyn agreed.

It had felt like Ashlyn and Kenner were criticizing Marin's family, like they had come into her house and only noticed crumbs and handprints and rips and stains.

Kenner had even said the stained glass in the church's sanctuary was ugly. How could anyone hate stained glass?

Ashlyn and Kenner won't be at this VBS, Marin told herself.

But neither would anyone else Marin knew. Marin would be the outsider here, the new kid. She'd be the one who didn't know the songs and didn't have any friends to partner with during games.

It'd be bad enough in the fall when school started, and she was the new kid there. But at school, teachers usually assigned kids to group projects, rather than letting anyone choose. At school, there'd probably be other new kids, and surely at least one of them would be as desperate for a friend as Marin was.

Going to this church's VBS would be like crashing somebody else's family reunion.

Marin thought about the three girls she'd seen that morning in matching striped sundresses. She couldn't go to VBS with them. She couldn't.

"That's . . . really nice of the church, to make that offer,"

Marin said faintly. Her brain raced. What excuse could she give for saying no that Dad would accept? "But . . . you keep saying that it's really good you're not on any schedule this summer, since Owen's sleeping and waking up is so . . . what's that word you and Mom keep using? Erratic? If you had to drive me to that church at a certain time and pick me up at a certain time, wouldn't that be a problem with Owen?"

"We could make it work," Dad said. But doubt had crept into his voice.

"Really, it's okay, Dad," Marin said. "I'd rather have you and Mom and Owen get as much sleep as you can, than go to that VBS. Because I want to be able to brag that my dad climbed Mount Everest!" She forced her mouth into the widest grin possible, hoping it was enough to trick Dad. "I can always go to VBS next summer."

Dad reached out and ruffled her hair.

"When did you get so mature and understanding?" he asked. "I'm sure Owen's sleep schedule will be more normal next summer. I hope. Regardless, I'm sure we'll know lots of other families by then, and we'll be able to carpool. . . . We might even have this house put together by then!"

"Yeah, by next summer, everything will be perfect." Marin laughed, and Dad joined in.

He didn't see through her excuse. He didn't understand at all.

By next summer, would she have figured out what was going on with the Remarkables? Or with Charley Schmidt?

Are you kidding? she thought as she lifted Owen out of the baby carrier and handed him to Dad. *If I can, I'm going to solve those mysteries tomorrow!*

At least she was going to try.

EIGHTEEN

The next afternoon, as soon as Owen went down for his nap, Marin raced back to Charley's clubhouse. She knocked on the door so hard that it swung open on its own.

"Oh, sorry," she started to say, sure that he'd be angry. "I didn't mean to . . ."

But the clubhouse was deserted, its beanbag chairs smashed against the walls as though someone had kicked them. She tiptoed toward the table in the middle of the room, already feeling guilty about trespassing.

He knows I saw his drawings yesterday, she told herself. *Would he really mind that much if I looked again today?*

She knew it was wrong, but she wanted to look *so* badly. Somehow it had started to seem like living in Pennsylvania would never feel right until she understood the Remarkables. And Charley Schmidt clearly knew a lot more about them than she did.

"I just want to help," she said aloud, as though Charley

were right there to hear her.

But when she reached the table in the middle of the room, it looked different. Someone—undoubtedly Charley—had wrapped a bicycle chain around the handle of the drawer, and attached the chain to one of the table legs.

It was wound so tightly that there was no way anyone could slip the chain down and over the bottom of the table leg. It was wound so tightly that no one could so much as peek into the drawer without knowing the combination to the lock.

"Okay, okay! I won't look!" she said. "I'll solve this on my own, and you'll feel sorry when *I* share what I know with *you*! When *I'm* the generous one!"

It was probably a bad sign that she was talking to someone who wasn't even there. Or, talking to herself, really. Wasn't that what crazy people did?

Or was it just what people did when they didn't have any friends?

An ache started in her throat, an ache that felt like it had been there waiting for her ever since things had started going wrong back in Illinois.

Maybe she wasn't really a friend-type person. Maybe Ashlyn wouldn't have even started being friends with her, way back in preschool, if it hadn't been for their parents all being friends first. And then Kenner was just friends with Marin because she became friends with Ashlyn.

It was like Marin had just inherited all the friends she'd ever had. It wasn't like she'd ever *earned* one of her own.

Marin whirled around and ran out of the clubhouse. She crashed through the woods, not even bothering to look for any path. Branches lashed against her face, and twigs scratched her arms, and she didn't care. She just raced straight toward the Remarkables' house.

She burst into the clearing of their backyard, not caring if anyone saw her. If someone did, she'd just blurt out all her questions at once: *Who are you? Where did you get your superpowers? Is something awful going to happen, like Charley said?*

A flicker of movement on the patio caught her eye, but by the time she turned her head to look directly, whatever it was had vanished.

Maybe it had just been a heat mirage, the shimmering of light that only happened on really hot days.

It wasn't that hot today. It was only June.

Maybe it was one or more of the Remarkables disappearing. Maybe if she'd been a split second earlier, she would have seen them.

If they're time travelers, like Charley said, then they're going from one time period to another when they disappear. From now back to . . . twenty years ago?

But why?

Marin decided to march up to the back door and knock. If anybody answered besides one of the Remarkables, she'd say . . . she'd say she was selling Girl Scout cookies. Or taking preorders, anyway.

But when Marin reached the edge of the patio, she saw that small square papers were scattered across the patio table. No, not papers—pictures. The old-fashioned kind you peeled off straight from the camera. Polaroids—was that what they were called?

Marin had seen Polaroids from when her parents were kids, and the pictures had gone smoky around the edges, the colors blurred, as if the image were sliding back into dust. Or into the past.

These Polaroids were crisp and clear, as if the pictures had just been taken.

Or as if Marin herself had traveled back into the past to look at them.

Practically holding her breath, she leaned close to study them, one after the other. But she was careful not to touch anything, because, however substantial the photos looked, it seemed like they might vanish if she tried to lift them up. She even held her ponytail back out of the way so her hair didn't brush the shimmery surfaces.

The first picture was of the Remarkables' backyard glowing with miniature lights, as if it were decorated for Christmas. *No, not Christmas,* Marin corrected herself. *A birthday.*

She could tell, because the picture included the edge of a homemade banner—created from an old bedsheet, maybe, but made by someone with as much artistic talent as a professional sign maker. The lettering was neat and precise, and said, *Happy 17th Birthday, M—*

Marin almost groaned with the frustration of not being able to see the whole name.

But one of the Remarkables has the same first initial I do! she thought jubilantly. *At least I know that much!*

She tried to think of *M* names a teenager from twenty years ago might have: Molly? Megan? Max? Mike?

There were so many *M* names. It was ridiculous to try to guess. Marin switched her attention to the next photo.

This Polaroid showed three of the Remarkables crowded into a single frame. The picture was taken sideways, as if they'd wanted the same effect as a selfie. (Had selfies existed twenty years ago?) All three of these Remarkables were laughing; just looking at the picture made Marin want to laugh, too. Everyone looked so happy. The boy in the middle had his hand raised to make bunny ears above the head of the girl beside him, and she had her face turned to the side because she knew what he was doing, and even though she was pushing him away, she seemed to think it was the biggest joke ever.

That girl had red hair—was she the one Marin had decided should be named Sunny or Sunshine or something like that? She was even prettier close up. Her freckles glowed just as much as the miniature lights in the first picture.

The other girl in the picture had beautiful long dark hair and brown skin. Her hair tumbled and whipped around, as if she'd been caught in the act of shaking her head at the other two Remarkables' antics. But she also had her arm raised— maybe *she'd* been about to make bunny ears behind the boy's head? Or maybe fake fangs by her own mouth?

The boy in the middle was laughing the hardest. He had brown hair cropped so short that it was barely more than fuzz, and brown eyes that crinkled at the corners. He looked like someone who laughed a lot. But that wasn't what made Marin stare and stare. Something about him seemed almost familiar, as if Marin should recognize the laughing eyes, the jutting chin, the nose with a little bump in the middle.

Charley said the Remarkables are from twenty years ago, so think about someone with that face who's an adult now, Marin told herself. *He'd be in his thirties now. So would he have wrinkles? Serious laugh lines? And remember, by now he could have grown his hair out or even gone bald like Dad. . . .*

Marin put a hand partly over her eyes so she could block her view of the boy's hair, and only look at his face. Marin had barely met any adult men in Summitview. There'd been the old man who'd given them the tour at church and . . . that was pretty much it.

Even if she expanded to thinking about males in general

that she'd met in Summitview, that was only the toddler she'd seen on Mrs. Jean Schmidt's swing set, and the baby Oliver in the crying room at the church. And Charley himself, of course.

Marin let out a gasp and jerked back so quickly she had to grab the patio table to keep her balance. Her hand brushed the edge of the Polaroid.

Instantly all of the pictures disappeared without a trace, as if they'd never been there in the first place.

But Marin barely noticed, because she'd taken off running again. She ran straight back to her own house, grabbed a pen and paper, then raced to Charley's clubhouse.

All that running at top speed left her out of breath and sweaty and panting, but she didn't pause. She spread the paper out on the table in the middle of Charley's clubhouse and began to write:

I know the secret of who you think the Remarkables are. Because one of them looks so much like you. It's your father, right?

Is your mother there, too? Did something bad happen to them both?

Don't you think, if time travel is possible and something awful is going to happen with the Remarkables . . . don't you think we can stop it?

NINETEEN

Marin spent a long time standing beside Charley's table, as if she had to watch over the note she'd written. She started to scratch out **something awful is going to happen** to make it into **something awful happened twenty years ago**, but then she scratched out the change instead.

If time travel were possible, then verb tenses were useless. Past and future could be the same.

Anyhow, Charley was more likely to believe her—more likely to think that they could change anything—if she could get him to think about the "something awful" as something in the future.

After a moment, she added two more sentences, one begging, **Call me as soon as you see this note!** and the other giving her phone number.

Her hand shook, gripping the pen, and she had to check and double-check to make sure she'd written the right numerals. She felt almost feverish with excitement—too buzzy and weird to think straight. Maybe that was how Charley had felt ever since he'd discovered the Remarkables. How weird would it be to see your own parents as they were as teenagers?

How much weirder would it be if you hadn't seen them in real life for the past five years?

She remembered how Charley had said, "Not *really*," in that odd way when he talked about not seeing his parents. Did he mean he'd only seen them as time travelers, not for real?

Marin struggled to think what could have happened, that Charley hadn't seen his parents for so long. Was it maybe the "something awful" he'd talked about with the Remarkables?

No, that doesn't make sense, because he said the Remarkables are time travelers from twenty years ago. Charley wasn't even alive then. . . .

The more Marin tried to answer one question, the more that dozens of others crowded into her mind to take its place.

Had Charley ever tried to *talk* to the Remarkables? Was that possible?

Marin bent forward, bracing her hands against her legs. She felt dizzy, and it wasn't just because she'd run so much and still hadn't caught her breath. She wanted Charley to materialize out of thin air—as if he himself were one of the Remarkables—so she could talk to him about everything she'd figured out and everything she still wondered.

How could he have kept all this secret ever since he was nine?

Or . . . had he actually kept it secret? Had he told anyone else?

If he had, Marin wanted to hunt up that person (or those people) and talk to them, because Charley *wasn't* materializing out of thin air. And for all Marin knew, it could be days before he came back to the clubhouse and saw her note.

A breeze blew through the clubhouse, swirling down from the broken section of the roof. It lifted Marin's note from the table and whirled the paper toward the cracks in the wall.

Marin hadn't even thought about the possibility of the note blowing away and Charley never seeing it.

Marin grabbed the paper and went outside to pick up pebbles and one large chunk of bark from the ground. She used those to anchor it firmly back on the table.

"It'd take a tornado to blow it away now," she said out loud.

She wondered if Charley was hiding nearby right now, and he could hear her talking to herself.

"Charley? Charley, are you there?" she called. "Don't you want to hear what I figured out? What I noticed about the Remarkables just now? What I think we can *do*?"

Silence.

Actually, that wasn't exactly true. Marin could hear the wind picking up again, whispering through the trees outside and whistling mournfully through the broken side of the clubhouse. She could hear birds tweeting and some sort of creature—a squirrel? a chipmunk? something small, anyway— scampering through the thick layer of leaves on the ground outside.

But she couldn't hear what she was straining her ears for, what she longed for most: an answer from Charley.

What if he wouldn't talk to her even after reading her note?

What if he never did?

TWENTY

"If you could travel through time and go anywhere you wanted, where would you want to go?" Marin asked Mom and Dad that night at the dinner table.

They were having spaghetti with sauce from a jar and salad out of a bag and garlic bread that came out of a box in the freezer. As Dad, Mom, and Marin had put it all out on the table, Dad had apologized, "I know it *seems* like we've had this every night since we moved here, but let me remind you, we did have that really good lasagna from Mrs. Jean Schmidt for two meals, and then we ordered Chinese that one time. . . . And someday maybe I'll be awake and alert enough to think about dinner *before* fifteen minutes ahead. . . ."

And Mom had answered with a jaw-splitting yawn and a pat on his arm, "Don't worry. I'm not awake enough to taste anything anyway."

Now they both blinked at Marin for a long time before either of them answered.

"See, Ellen," Dad finally said to Mom, "that's exactly the kind of intellectually challenging conversation starters we should talk about every night at dinner. Didn't we used to talk about lofty concepts like that back when we got real sleep at night?"

"So . . . you're saying you'd want to go to a time when you could sleep all you want?" Marin asked.

Dad put down his fork and rubbed his hand over his bald head.

"So tempting," he admitted. "But, wow, does that ever make me sound boring." He tightened his grip on Owen, who was asleep nestled against Dad's left arm like a football. "And no way would I do that, if it meant having to trade Owen for a good night's sleep." He playfully punched Marin in the arm. "Or *you,* pipsqueak! You kept us awake all the time when you were a baby, too."

"Partly that was because when you fell asleep, we'd sit there watching you and admiring how cute you were, instead of taking every chance to sleep ourselves," Mom said. "At least we've learned not to do that so much with Owen."

She yawned again.

"So I guess you'd just fast-forward to a time when Owen is sleeping through the night so you can, too," Marin said.

"*No,*" Mom said, a little too sharply. "How could we miss every little phase and all the miraculous changes Owen is going to make over the next days or weeks or months until that happens?"

"Oh, please, God, let it be just days, not weeks or months. Or years," Dad said, pressing the palms of his hands together and rolling his eyes upward as though he was praying. Maybe he was, just a little jokingly.

Dad did everything jokingly.

Mom laughed and gently stroked the fine hairs sticking up on Owen's head. Owen smiled in his sleep, and Mom's face softened. She didn't look so tired anymore. She looked more like someone watching a miracle.

"Yeah, yeah, I get it that you love Owen—" Marin began.

"And you," Dad interrupted.

"Okay, both of us. And each other," Marin added quickly, because Mom and Dad could get so mushy sometimes. "But, really, let's say you could travel through time. Wouldn't you want to fix some mistake in history? Or . . . or some mistake you'd made?"

Marin took too big of a gulp of air. This was pretty much the closest she'd ever come to telling Mom and Dad about what happened with Ashlyn and Kenner back in Illinois. And she couldn't do that. They couldn't ever know. They'd be so ashamed of her.

"What?" Dad asked with mock indignation. "You think *I've* ever made a mistake? My entire life has led to this moment, where I've got the most incredible wife in the world, the most incredible daughter in the world, the most incredible son in the world—how could anything that led to this be a mistake?"

He whipped his head back and forth, peering at first Mom, then Marin, then Owen. He pushed his eyebrows up as high as they could go, and he let his jaw drop and his cheeks go slack so they flapped a little. This was his "I'm a cartoon character" expression that he used sometimes in his classes when kids were bouncing off the walls and not listening. He made the kids guess which character he was supposed to be, and no matter what they said, he told them they were right.

"Your father is clearly delirious," Mom said, rolling her eyes. "My brain's not firing on all cylinders either, but I did actually take a science fiction class way back in college, and I remember the professor wanting us to think about this question really, really seriously. You go back and try to fix a problem in time, and what if you end up just creating other problems instead? Or—worse ones?"

"Yeah, what if you tried to stop John Wilkes Booth from assassinating Abraham Lincoln, and somehow that made it so your mom and I never met?" Dad asked.

"How *would* you stop that assassination?" Mom asked. "I'm just curious."

"Oh, I'd tackle John Wilkes Booth outside Ford's Theatre, then truss him up like a chicken in some handy-dandy ropes

I'd borrow from the stage crew—I mean, just look at these muscles I've developed carrying Owen around," Dad said, flexing a bicep. "I wouldn't even break a sweat."

Marin tried to imagine what she'd do with Ashlyn and Kenner, if she could go back in time and stop everything that had happened before it even started. That would be such a relief.

The first time Kenner was mean to me, the first time Ashlyn was mean to me, what I should have done was . . .

It was almost a full year since the problems had started. How could Marin still not know what she should have done?

And it's just a few more months until school starts here. What if . . . what if I still don't know how to deal with friends then?

A loud dinging sounded, and Mom, Dad, and Marin all jumped. Owen woke up and started crying.

"Whoa—didn't realize the doorbell would sound so loud from the kitchen table," Dad said, swinging Owen back and forth in his arms to try to soothe him. "I think I need to put that on the list of things to adjust once there's time. Which . . . might be about the time Owen turns ten."

"I forget," Mom said. "How long do you have to live in a new place before you stop discovering new surprises?"

"I'll get the door," Marin said, because she was suddenly seized with hope. Could it be Charley at the door? Had he read her note and been so eager to talk to her that he came right over?

Marin raced to the front door and pulled it open—and no one was there.

Are the Remarkables going around the neighborhood ringing doorbells and then disappearing as soon as someone answers? she wondered.

That made them seem more like ghosts than time travelers.

That made them seem scary.

Then Marin noticed that the bush at the side of the house was shaking, as though someone had just run past it.

She stepped down onto the front porch, ready to chase after whoever it was. But she was barefoot—she'd kicked off her flip-flops right before dinner because Owen had spit up on them, and she'd had to wash them and they were right now drying by the back door. Her toes brushed against something that was softer than the concrete of the front porch.

Paper. Thick, folded-over paper, maybe?

Marin looked down, and there was an envelope labeled in a messy scrawl: *FOR MARIN.*

The envelope was held in place by a large, flat stone, and that made Marin grin. This had to be from Charley. And he'd borrowed her idea of anchoring the note she'd left for him.

Is that like . . . agreeing? she wondered.

She bent down and snatched up the envelope. He'd sealed

the back, so she had to rip it open. And then he'd folded the letter inside, down to just one narrow strip, so unfolding it seemed to take forever.

But finally she had the paper flattened out and she could make sense of the words: first, a large, shaky, *YES*, then in smaller print, *Meet me at 2 p.m. tomorrow. You know where.*

TWENTY-ONE

"Really, all you had to do was *call*," Marin said.

It was the next afternoon, and she had just stepped into Charley's clubhouse. He stood on the other side of the table, as far away as he could and still be in the clubhouse with her. It was weird—it was like neither one of them knew what to say, or how they should act, now that they were facing each other.

"No, I couldn't," Charley said. He kicked at the nearest beanbag chair, sending it sliding across the floor. "I don't have my own phone, remember?"

"But doesn't your grandma—"

"I told you, she's old-fashioned," Charley said. "Her phone is still a landline, and it's actually *attached* to the wall in the kitchen. So if I want to make a phone call, I pretty much have to stand there in front of her. Or in front of my brothers. And they're all normal, you know? Not anything like me. Everyone else in my house is normal, and they fill the house with normal, and that makes it so I don't belong there, and that's why I have to stay outside all the time, and—"

"You don't think you're normal, too?" Marin asked.

Charley tilted his head, letting his hair fall over his face.

"I can see people the way they were twenty years ago," he said. "I see things that happened before I was even born."

"Well, so do I," Marin said. "*I* think that makes us better than normal. Like, we're special!"

Why did she sound so much like Dad all of a sudden?

"Yeah, sure." Charley frowned in a way that hurt to watch. "And that's why I go to a *special* school. Special isn't good. Normal is."

Who did he sound like?

Oh, right, Marin thought, her heart sinking. *Kenner.*

Before she'd met Kenner, Marin never thought about what was normal and what wasn't. She'd liked being herself. She'd been so proud that Dad was the gym teacher at *her* school; she'd been so proud of the way he made kids laugh and laugh and laugh, all the time.

She'd also liked how excited her science teacher, Mr. Wu, got talking about plants, and how her language arts teacher, Ms. Condi, did special voices when she read books out loud. Before Kenner, Marin had never even noticed Mr. Wu's hair or Ms. Condi's makeup.

She'd also never worried that having food stuck in her own teeth might make someone not want to talk to her.

Or not want to be her friend.

"Some advice for you," Charley said. "Don't tell anyone about seeing the Remarkables. Not unless you want to get stuck going to a special school, too. And having to see therapists and counselors who don't even understand."

"You *told*?" Marin asked. "Did any adults . . . help? Have any *adults* seen the Remarkables?"

She imagined a bunch of scientists in special germproof uniforms swarming around the Remarkables' house, filming their every appearance and disappearance, maybe using special instruments to measure . . . what would it be called? Sightings? *Disturbances*? Disturbances in the fabric of time?

Charley snorted.

"You think any adult went and *looked*?" he asked. "They just said I was *troubled*. Or, if they were trying to sound nice, that I had 'quite an imagination.' And that I shouldn't think it was my fault that my parents . . . that my parents . . ." He coughed. "I was *nine*. Like I said, I was stupid back then. I said too much. I don't talk about the Remarkables *now*."

"What was it about your parents that . . . ," Marin began cautiously.

Charley's face hardened. It was like watching a door slam. He might as well have thrown her out of the clubhouse right then.

"I want to help!" Marin protested. "Remember, I *have*

seen the Remarkables, too. I know you're not making it up or going crazy. Or, if you're crazy, I'm crazy, too. I just want to know what's going on!"

Charley winced. He kept his head down, avoiding her gaze.

"I don't want you to know about my parents," he whispered. "I'm ashamed."

"Because of something that happened twenty years ago?" Marin asked. "Before you were even born?"

Now Charley looked up, but he still wouldn't look at her. His eyes focused behind her.

He was staring at the door.

"Somebody died twenty years ago," he said. "A girl. And it was my father's fault."

In spite of everything she tried to do to stop herself, Marin shivered. Shivers didn't usually make any noise, but maybe this one did. Or maybe she let out a little gasp, too. Charley jerked his head to the side, so now he was staring straight at her.

This is a test, Marin thought. *What I say next could change everything.*

She forced herself to stand up straighter, and drill her gaze right back at Charley's eyes.

"So we know what we have to do if we can learn how to travel through time like the Remarkables," Marin said. "We have to save that girl's life."

TWENTY-TWO

Charley went back to avoiding Marin's gaze.

"You don't even know the story," he protested. "You don't know what you're talking about."

Marin felt jittery and impatient, but she forced herself to bend her knees and sprawl casually into one of the beanbag chairs. If she were sitting down, wouldn't that make it harder for Charley to order her out?

"Then tell me," she said.

Charley hovered, as if he wanted to sit down, too, but wasn't sure how sitting worked.

"Which story do you want?" he asked. "Mine? My dad's? The other Remarkables'?"

"All of them," Marin said.

Charley sighed. He slumped down into the beanbag chair beside Marin's.

"There were a lot of kids in this neighborhood when my dad was in high school," Charley began in a flat voice, as if he could tell the story only if he made it nothing but a collection of facts.

"Did your mother grow up in this neighborhood, too?" Marin asked.

Charley frowned at her.

"Yeah. But that doesn't matter yet."

Yet? Marin thought.

"Grandma says, in every neighborhood, there's a house that just becomes the place where everyone hangs out," Charley said. He started picking at the seam of his beanbag chair, as if he planned to work the plastic threads loose. "At least, Grandma says that's how it used to be, before cell phones and video games."

"And in this neighborhood, when your parents were in high school . . . ," Marin prompted.

"In our neighborhood, the high school hangout was *that* house," Charley finished for her. "Where we've both seen the Remarkables."

"Okay," Marin said. "That makes sense. Who lived there?"

"A girl named Missy. Melissa Caravechio."

An M name! Marin thought. *So was it her birthday sign I saw?*

Charley stood up and walked stiffly, almost robotically, toward the table. He pulled out the drawer—Marin saw that it wasn't locked anymore—and he came back with a stack of drawings. He sat back down and leafed through them before pulling one out and handing it to Marin.

It was a drawing of a girl with bright red hair and freckles—the girl Marin had seen that first day in a yellow skirt, when Marin had decided the girl should be named Sunny or Sunshine, or something like that.

"That's her," Charley said.

"Melissa Caravechio," Marin repeated.

"Grandma says Missy's dad was Italian but her mom was Irish, and that's why she had that red hair," Charley said. He looked down at his hands. "And my dad had this huge, huge crush on Missy, starting when they were in about second grade. Grandma says, if my dad could have, he would have spent every waking moment over at her house."

"Okay," Marin said. "So were they . . . dating?"

It felt funny to say the word *dating* to a boy. It made her think of playing Barbie dolls with Ashlyn when they were little kids. Ashlyn had said if the Ken doll and one of the Barbie dolls drove around in the Barbie car together, that was a date.

It also made her think of the beginning of fifth grade, when Kenner had looked around at the other kids in their new classroom and said, "Which boy would you want to go with? I like Simon, so you can't say him. He's mine! I've got dibs!"

So *go with* were the right words, not *dating*.

Marin felt her face flush. But Charley was talking about

high school kids twenty years ago, not fifth graders last fall, so maybe *dating* really was what she meant.

Charley shook his head.

"Missy's parents were really strict," he said. "They said she wasn't allowed to have a boyfriend until she turned seventeen."

Seventeen, Marin thought.

In her mind's eye she could summon the picture she'd seen at the Remarkables' house—at Missy Caravechio's house—of the decorated backyard and the sign *Happy 17th Birthday, M*—

That had been a picture from a party for Missy for a very important birthday. Everything was coming together.

Marin felt jubilant, as if she herself had been invited to a party, as if she herself were going to get to hang out with sunshiny Missy Caravechio and Charley's laughing dad and the girl with the beautiful long dark hair.

Then she remembered that someone had died. A girl. Which one?

"How—" she began.

Charley waved away the question. He bent his head down to stare at the floor.

"There was a party when Missy turned seventeen," he said, his voice robotic again. "And Grandma says it wasn't some wild, out-of-control-teenagers type of thing. She said she was there, and my grandfather, because he hadn't had his heart attack yet, and other neighbors, and lots of Missy's aunts and uncles and cousins . . . Family and friends of all ages. And you know, the Caravechios' house wasn't that big. So people were packed in tight, and they kept bringing out more and more food—Grandma says the Irish side of the family and the Italian side of the family were kind of competing to have the most of *their* kind of food on the table. And . . . have you ever had Totino's pizza rolls, or are your parents the kind who make you eat healthy all the time?"

"Totino's pizza rolls . . . what?" Marin recoiled, and shook her head as if to clear it. Had she heard him wrong? "I mean, sure, I've had pizza rolls, but what's that got to do with anything?"

"Grandma says my dad had this running joke with Missy, that she was too authentically Italian to eat fake Italian food like Chef Boyardee or frozen pizza. Or Totino's. So as part of that joke, at Missy's birthday party, my dad put a tray of Totino's pepperoni pizza rolls into the oven."

Charley was staring more intently at the floor than ever. Why? And why was he slowing his voice down, as if he were talking about some horrible crime instead of just food?

"And right away, the oven started to smoke," Charley said.

Charley's gaze was locked on the floor so tightly now that Marin half expected to see *it* start to smoke, as if he'd developed laser vision or X-ray vision, something like that.

"The smoke could have just been from ice crystals on the

cookie tray, or crumbs from the pizza rolls that dropped off onto the bottom of the oven," Charley said. "There was nothing really *wrong*. But my dad started to worry that he was going to set off the smoke detector, and everyone would have to run out of the house to get away from the noise, and . . . and that would ruin the party. And he didn't want to ruin anything, not when he was hoping Missy would agree to be his girlfriend by the end of the night. So he went out into the hallway and pulled over a chair and . . . he took the batteries out of the smoke detector."

Charley stopped talking, as if he expected Marin to figure out the rest.

"I guess . . . there was a fire then?" Marin whispered.

Finally, Charley turned his head to look at her. His face was stony-blank, as if he'd put up some sort of guard to avoid any feelings.

"Yes." He winced. Maybe he wasn't good at avoiding anything. "The house was hit by lightning a week later. Missy's parents woke up to find the whole house in flames, and they barely made it out. They couldn't understand why the smoke detector hadn't warned them. And they couldn't get back in to rescue Missy. And she died in her sleep. All because of my dad and his stupid joke."

TWENTY-THREE

"No, it was because of the lightning starting the fire," Marin said. Hearing Charley sound so glum and hopeless made her want to argue. It was almost like how she'd always wanted to argue with Kenner and Ashlyn those last few months in Illinois, whenever she thought they were making fun of her, giggling together, and then saying, *Oh, nothing*, every time she asked what they were laughing about.

Or sometimes they said, *You wouldn't understand.*

Was Marin just becoming the type of person who wanted to argue about everything?

She was right about the lightning and the fire. She needed Charley to see that.

"It was the *fire* that killed that girl," Marin repeated. "It wasn't like your dad murdered her or anything. He didn't *want* her to die."

"Nobody can control lightning, though," Charley said. "All we can control is how we react to a natural tragedy like that. Or how we prepare for it. And my dad always felt like, if he had never taken those batteries out, or if he'd remembered to put them back in, the smoke detector would have worked, and Missy would have heard it and escaped. And survived."

It almost felt like he was quoting someone. An adult. Maybe his grandma again.

"Why did your grandma even tell you that story?" Marin asked. "It's so horrible, and it makes your dad sound like— like . . . like someone bad. When all he was doing was trying to play a joke at a party."

Charley twisted his hands together. He bit his lip.

"My dad *is* someone bad," he murmured. He looked down again. "No matter what anyone says. Grandma told me that story so I'd know how it all started. How it snowballed from Dad just feeling so guilty after Missy died to him doing all sorts of other bad things to . . . to try to kill the pain. She wanted me to know that he hadn't always been a terrible person. And . . . to forgive him."

"You have, haven't you?" Marin asked. "He wasn't *trying* to hurt anyone! It was just a joke!"

"Not the rest of what he did," Charley said. "What he did after. For the past twenty years."

Marin waited, but Charley didn't explain.

"Okay, okay," Marin said. "At least we know that what we need to do to save Missy Caravechio is simple. Batteries.

Smoke detector. Done!"

"Sure," Charley said, though he sounded so glum he might as well have said, *You're totally wrong.* "Except we'd have to fix the smoke detector during the one week that passed between the party and the lightning strike, and it all happened twenty years ago. . . . I've been watching that house and the Remarkables for almost two years now, and I've never once seen a calendar or heard anyone say what month it is, let alone a particular day or week. Nobody even says the year. When *you* saw the Remarkables, did you know what date it was?"

Marin opened her mouth to say, *It was the first day we moved into our house, so that was June the . . . uh . . .*

Then she understood what he meant. If seeing the Remarkables meant she was seeing the past, or seeing them *traveling* from the past, it didn't matter at all what the date was for her. It could be June for her and any month at all for them.

"Did you ever try going *into* the Remarkables' house to look for a calendar?" she asked. "Or peeking in their windows? Surely . . ."

Something else struck her.

"Wait a minute. If Missy Caravechio's house burned down twenty years ago, how is there still a house there now?" she asked. "Are we seeing a whole *house* that traveled from the past? Or is it a different house? A newer one?"

She was making herself feel more and more as though the Remarkables were ghosts, not time travelers.

That made them scarier.

Except, they couldn't be ghosts if Missy Caravechio was the only one of them who was dead.

Was she the only one who was dead?

"It's a new house," Charley said. "But it's a lot like the old house—one story, with a porch at the front, and a patio at the back. . . . I think sometimes it shifts, and I see the old house instead. For years and years and years, there wasn't anything there. It was just an empty lot, because Missy's parents were too heartbroken to rebuild. Grandma says they moved away and never came back. And then almost two years ago, I was playing in the woods by myself, and I broke through into the clearing, and someone had started building a new house. And then the sunlight around the house changed somehow—well, it's hard to explain, if—"

"No, I understand!" Marin exclaimed, practically bouncing up and down. "Everything you were seeing kind of glowed, right? Like the light wasn't just coming from overhead, but from everywhere around you. And then you saw the Remarkables, I bet, and it was all just . . . amazing. Wasn't it?"

It was a relief that she didn't have to worry about explaining everything right. Clearly she and Charley had had the same experience.

"Yeah . . ." Charley did not seem to share her excitement. "I guess you do know what it's like. So maybe you understand why, when I'm watching the Remarkables, I'm not thinking about the differences between the new and the old house. I'm just trying not to break the spell." He gave a disgusted snort. "Except, that first time, I wanted to show other people, too. I was totally freaked out, I guess, and that made Grandma freak out, and next thing you know, everybody's so, so worried about me. Because no one could see what I saw."

"But I do," Marin said.

Charley shrugged, but it was a slow shrug, one that wasn't completely hopeless.

Marin looked past him to the stack of drawings he'd laid down beside the beanbag chair. The Remarkables were smiling or laughing in every picture she could see.

So every time Charley saw them, it had to have been before the fire, she thought. *Before their story turned sad.*

But at the Remarkables' house she'd seen a photo, at least, from the day of Missy's seventeenth birthday party. What if they were getting closer and closer to the tragedy? What if they didn't have much time?

"When you were telling me the story, you kept saying what your Grandma told you," Marin said hesitantly. "Did you ever hear about Missy straight from your dad? Or . . . your mom?"

"Don't tell me I need to go talk to my parents!" Charley protested. "I won't!"

"Okay!" Marin said, hoping that was enough to calm him down. "I just wondered . . . your grandma seems really nice and everything, but what if . . . what if there are parts of the story she didn't tell you? Or . . . it was a long time ago. What if she just didn't remember everything right? Or what if there were important details she never knew?" Marin hoped it didn't sound like she was attacking Mrs. Jean Schmidt. She just didn't want to believe anything bad about any of the Remarkables. "I mean . . ."

Charley was already shaking his head. Shaking his head—and reaching under the beanbag beside him.

"I know Grandma told me the story right," he said. "Because I found this under a floorboard in my bedroom. Which . . . used to be my dad's bedroom when he was a teenager."

Charley pulled out a thin box that said *Finest Stationery* in fancy script on the top. But when he lifted the lid, Marin didn't see blank sheets of fancy paper and envelopes. She saw old yellowing newspaper clippings with screaming headlines: *LOCAL GIRL DIES IN TRAGIC HOUSE FIRE* and *SMOKE DETECTOR FAILS TO SOUND . . .*

With shaking hands, Marin picked up the top newspaper story and gingerly unfolded it.

There've got to be pictures, she thought. *And pictures*

would prove . . . everything.

A large, black-rimmed rectangle hung above the *TRAGIC HOUSE FIRE* headline. It was clearly the space where there had once been a photo. But Marin couldn't even tell if the photo was of the burning house or the ashes of the house or some memorial to Melissa Caravechio. Because someone had covered over the entire picture with the same two words scrawled over and over and over again in thick black marker: *my fault my fault my fault my fault my fault my fault my fault. . . .*

TWENTY-FOUR

"Your dad's the one who should have gone to see a therapist," Marin said, letting the newspaper clipping drop back into the box. "I mean, a therapist, or a psychologist, or a minister or a priest—someone who would have helped him."

"Grandma said she tried to make him do that, to talk to *someone*," Charley said. He was back to sounding matter-of-fact. "But he said nothing helped. Except . . ."

"Except what?"

Charley looked like he regretted saying that much.

"Charley, I'm trying to help here! I don't even know your dad, so it's not like I would tell him what you said, or—"

"Drugs," Charley said. "He started using drugs. And then my mom did, too. Because he made her unhappy, too. And they wouldn't stop. And that's why Brandon, Brady, and I live with Grandma."

Charley's face was red. But he took a deep breath and let it out, and Marin stayed silent. And then he said, "You know what? It wasn't as hard to tell you that as I thought."

"Because you can trust me," Marin said. "Remember? I see people who aren't there, too." Her voice was a little shaky—and, strangely, even her knees felt shaky. But she forced herself to reach out and pat Charley's shoulder.

It was a motion that felt oddly familiar.

Oh, she realized. *It's what I've seen Dad do a million times with kids who are upset at school. And when I was little and Dad used to take me to see Mom at the hospital where she worked, I'd see her doing that with her patients. I'm being like Mom and Dad!*

What would it be like to be Charley, with parents he *didn't* want to imitate?

With parents he was ashamed of?

"And we're going to work together," Marin said. She could tell she was sounding a little too cheerful again. "We'll fix everything for Missy Caravechio and your mom and dad!"

"But how?" Charley asked, spreading his hands wide.

There was that hopelessness again.

"I don't know—yet," Marin said. She reached for the box in Charley's arms. "Could I borrow this? Maybe if I read all the newspaper stories, that'll help. And then we can make a plan together."

"Sure," Charley said, closing the lid and slipping the box into her hands.

It was such a small box, and it contained nothing but old papers. But as Marin clutched it to her chest, it felt strangely heavy, as though every black scrawled *my fault my fault my fault* weighed a ton.

Looking at those words again and again, on one newspaper photo after another, would be painful. How had Charley ever borne looking at those words himself? When it was his own father who'd written them?

"No, you know what?" Marin said, changing her mind. "I think we should look at these articles as they were in the original newspaper. So we can see all the pictures, too. And who knows, maybe we'll see that something else happened that same day or that same week that helps us out. . . . Do you think we could find copies of those papers somewhere? At the library, maybe?"

She was really just trying to avoid seeing the words *my fault* any more than she had to. But Charley grinned.

"Did Grandma tell you how she used to be a public librarian?" he said, rolling his eyes. "She'll be so happy you got me out of the woods to go to the library. She'll love you forever!"

TWENTY-FIVE

In the end, Dad was the one who agreed to take Marin and Charley to the library in downtown Summitview.

First, there'd been a whole backyard conference between Dad and Mrs. Schmidt, figuring out when Owen was likeliest to nap next and when Mrs. Schmidt had to take Charley's younger brothers to baseball practice.

Then Dad and Marin made a quick pit stop back at the house so Dad could change out of his University of Illinois T-shirt with the dried Owen spit-up dribbled down the sleeve. As soon as they stepped inside the sliding glass door and shut it behind them, Dad gave Marin a playful shove on the shoulder.

"Look at you!" he marveled. "First of the Plucketts to make a friend in Summitview! You go, Marin! It didn't even take you a full week! And I didn't even know you'd met Charley, let alone started *planning* things together!"

"What? *No*," Marin said. "Charley isn't . . ."

She couldn't possibly explain that she and Charley weren't actually friends; they were just . . . not-normal . . . together. It was too hard to explain that their plans were all about something that had happened twenty years ago.

She couldn't ever explain about the Remarkables or Missy Caravechio or Charley's parents. It would feel too much like she was betraying Charley if she even tried.

Dad kept beaming proudly at her.

"You and Mom made friends before I did," Marin said, changing tacks. "With Mrs. Jean Schmidt, and all those people who sat around us at church on Sunday, and all the people Mom works with, and . . ."

Dad waved those examples away.

"They're still just new acquaintances," he said. "With the *possibility* of friendship, I'll grant you, but . . . nobody's invited us to go anywhere with them yet. Not for so much as an ice cream cone, let alone to the *library*." He kept the silly grin plastered on his face and leaned close. "Just between you and me, I don't think anybody's ever invited me to go to a library with them. Do you think it's that whole dumb-jock stereotype? If so, I resemble—I mean, *resent*—that suggestion!"

"Dad, you read a lot!" Marin protested. "And you're smart! Don't say that! Who's ever called you a dumb jock?"

Dad had his shirt over his face as he pulled it off.

"Never mind," he said, tossing the shirt into the laundry

room and pulling a new one out of the stack of clean, folded clothes that no one had remembered to take upstairs yet. "I should probably read more history and less about sports. So I have something to talk about in all those job interviews I'm going to get."

Was Dad worried that he hadn't gotten any calls for interviews yet? Was that what this was really about?

Dad finished pulling on the clean shirt. He reached over to muss Marin's hair.

"Maybe I'll look for some books of my own when we're at the library," he said, switching from mussing her hair to smoothing back the strands that had escaped from her ponytail. "Yeah, that's what I'll do. I'll drop you off, go pick up diapers for Owen, come back and check out a few books. . . . You and Charley don't mind staying at the library for a while, do you?"

"We need to," Marin said. "We've got a lot to—" She broke off and was glad that Dad seemed too distracted now to ask what she meant.

It was awkward in the minivan, with Marin and Charley sitting mostly in silence while Dad jabbered away about Summitview and his memories of summers when he was a kid, and how Pennsylvania was different from where they'd lived in Illinois or where he'd grown up in Indiana. Somehow Dad knew not to ask about Charley's parents or Charley's school—there were a couple close calls, where Dad *seemed* about to go in that direction, and then veered away. Dad did ask if Charley played baseball like his brothers, and Charley just kind of grunted, "No," and flashed a panicked look at Marin, as if to say, *Can't he tell I'm not like my brothers?*

And then Owen started crying in his car seat, and Dad stopped saying anything except "Shh, shh, Owen, just a few minutes more, we're almost there. . . . Marin, can you check to see if anything's actually wrong, or if he's just mad about being in the car?"

And Marin leaned over and whispered to Owen, "Once again, little dude, you are awesome! Good timing! But, really, you're fine, and you can stop crying now. . . ." And then Owen broke off mid-cry, as if he'd totally understood, and Marin couldn't help laughing.

"What happened?" Dad asked from the front seat. "Charley, did you see that? My own children are already ganging up on me. It's a conspiracy, I tell you—a kid-versus-adult conspiracy!"

And then they were at the library.

It was an imposing, old-fashioned building with stone arches and a soaring dome. When Dad dropped them off on the front sidewalk, Marin had a moment of wanting to turn around and call, "No, wait! Forget the library! Charley and I will just go to the grocery with you, Dad!"

It was almost like she thought the words *my fault my fault my fault* would be scrawled on the computer archives of the newspaper stories, too.

Beside her, Charley pulled a baseball cap out of his back pocket and tugged it over his hair and low over his eyes.

"What are you doing?" Marin asked. "Isn't there some rule about how guys are supposed to take baseball caps *off* when they go into a building, not put them on?"

Charley tilted his head toward her in a way that almost let her see his eyes.

"If I have this cap on, people will just think I'm a kid who doesn't know that rule," he said. "But if I take it off, all these little old ladies will come over to me and say, 'Oh, Charley! You've grown so much since I saw you last! How's your grandma doing? Tell her I said hi!' Or, they'll see what we're looking at, and they'll think, they'll think . . .'"

"Oh," Marin said. A second later, she added, "That's smart." And then, "You want me to do the talking?"

Charley nodded.

They mounted the stairs, opened the doors, and right away found a librarian standing under a sign that said *Got a Question? Ask It Here!*

To Marin's relief, this librarian wasn't one of the little old ladies Charley seemed so afraid of. Instead, this librarian was so young she could have practically fit in with the

Remarkables. And she had wild, curly hair dyed purple, which Marin liked.

"Sign-ups for the summer reading program are downstairs," she said automatically as Marin and Charley approached the desk. "Or *on*line, if you don't want to stand *in* line." She grinned in a goofy way that made Marin think even the librarian thought that was a corny way to put it. Like she was laughing *at* herself and *about* herself, all at once.

"Or—are you two old enough to be volunteers?" the librarian asked. "Oh, please say you're volunteers. We need you! Have you finished sixth grade or higher?"

Marin exchanged glances with Charley, though his eyes barely showed under the baseball cap.

"Just fifth, sorry," Marin said. "Maybe we'll volunteer next summer." It felt funny to say that. She couldn't even think about this summer ending, let alone how she was going to get through a whole school year to make it to next summer. "Actually, we're here for some research. I just moved to Summitview, and I want to learn about, uh, the town's history. Where can we find copies of old newspapers?"

The purple-haired librarian raised an eyebrow.

"How far back you want to go?" she asked. "Summitview was founded in 1762, but the first newspaper wasn't printed until . . . oh, drat, I can never remember exactly. I can look it up. But—"

"We just want to look at papers from twenty years ago," Marin said.

"Ouch," the librarian said. "I don't really think of that as history. That's when *I* was in fifth grade!"

Charley elbowed Marin and whispered, "So she wasn't one of the Remarkables. Too young," while the librarian peered at the computer screen.

Marin jolted. Whenever Charley was out and about in Summitview, he must look around constantly wondering which adults were the right age to have been in high school with his dad and Missy Caravechio.

Had Marin met any adults already who might have been Remarkables?

It was hard to think of the Remarkables as adults. Of course, it was also hard to think of adults as being kids once upon a time.

Had this purple-haired librarian wanted purple hair even way back when she was a fifth grader?

Marin decided it would probably be rude to ask.

The librarian straightened up.

"Okay, I can sign you on to one of the computers for the next hour. Come on over, and I'll show you how it all works." The three of them walked to a computer desk beside one of the windows, and the librarian pulled over an extra chair so both kids could sit down. The librarian called up the newspaper archives. "So you want twenty years ago. . . . Any particular date? Or any particular event you're looking for?"

"August third," Charley mumbled, and the librarian shot him a puzzled glance before typing it in.

The screen filled with the front page of the *Summitview Times* from that date. Half the page was filled with the story Charley had shown Marin before, the one with the headline *LOCAL GIRL DIES IN TRAGIC HOUSE FIRE.* But the picture Charley's dad had covered with the words *my fault my fault my fault* was clear and distinct here. The newspaper photographer had caught a moment when flames shot out of every window, and the roof was just starting to collapse. Sparks flew up like stars.

It was a beautiful photo, if you could make yourself forget that anyone had ever lived there.

Or died there.

"Oh, kiddos," the librarian murmured. "That's such a sad story. Are you sure you don't want to see some of the more *fun* parts of Summitview's history? I'm told the bicentennial celebration was really impressive. . . ."

"This happened in my neighborhood," Marin said stubbornly. "My family just moved in. . . ."

"Yeah, I get it," the librarian said. "I'm sure you've heard the neighbors talking already. . . . Not much happens in Summitview, so anything that does is remembered forever.

My great-aunt lived on that street. After that fire, she made us double-check to make sure her smoke detector was still working every time we visited."

Marin saw Charley stiffen beside her, but the librarian was already walking away.

Marin took control of the keyboard.

"Are you okay to do this?" she asked.

"Sure, why not? We're fixing everything, aren't we?" Charley mumbled in a rough voice that made it sound like he definitely wasn't okay.

Marin read every word on the front page. She was just about to turn the page to read the rest of the story, and see the "More pictures inside" promised at the bottom of the page, when her phone began vibrating in the pocket of her jeans shorts.

It was Dad.

"Marin, I'm sorry—I'm going to have to come back and pick you and Charley up right now," he said frantically into the phone when Marin answered. It didn't even sound like his voice. "You'll have to go back another day. . . ."

Was he crying?

"Dad, what's wrong?" Marin asked. She tried to make a joke, the way Dad would. "You sound like somebody died!"

"Oh, Marin," Dad moaned. "Somebody did!"

TWENTY-SIX

"Uncle Pete's not really my uncle," Marin said. She and Charley were outside on the sidewalk, watching for the minivan to come swinging around the corner. "He was my dad's best friend in college, and they both became gym teachers, and then Uncle Pete became a principal in the next town over from where we lived in Illinois. . . . Dad always said, 'All that stress, it's not for me! It'll kill you. . . .'"

Marin let her voice trail off. *Kill.* Uncle Pete had died unexpectedly—he'd been alive and seemed perfectly healthy one moment, and then been dead the next. No one knew yet if he'd had a heart attack or a stroke, or if something else had killed him. Was it possible that she might start to cry, just over that one word, *kill*? Uncle Pete was the closest person she'd ever known who had died. And he was the exact same age as her dad.

And she'd just been reading about someone dying.

But, really, Uncle Pete was more of an idea to her than a

person, because once he became a principal, he didn't have as much time to get together with Marin's dad as he used to. Marin probably hadn't seen Uncle Pete in four or five years. When Dad saw him, it was usually because one of Uncle Pete's sons was playing in some soccer tournament nearby, and Dad went to stand on the sidelines and cheer him on alongside Uncle Pete. Uncle Pete had had all sons—four boys. . . .

Four boys who don't have a father at all anymore, Marin thought.

Just thinking that made Marin feel weird. She was sad, anyway, for her dad, and of course for all of Uncle Pete's family. But she hardly remembered them. Should she feel even sadder than she actually did? Was there something wrong with her if she *didn't* want to cry?

None of it seemed real.

She was just glad that Charley didn't ask any questions.

Dad pulled up and they got into the minivan, and Dad barely grunted. That was the strangest thing of all—Dad not talking.

Even Owen was quiet, all the way home.

Dad turned into their own driveway and stopped. He shut off the engine and just sat there. His shoulders began to shake.

"Dad, do you want me to take Owen into the house?" Marin asked. "So you can . . ."

Keep sitting there? Keep crying?

She didn't know what she could say. Maybe she should pretend that Dad wasn't crying, that she didn't even notice—to give him some privacy.

She didn't know how to deal with any version of Dad that wasn't happy.

"Oh. Sure," Dad mumbled, as if he'd totally forgotten about Owen. Maybe about Marin, too.

Marin pulled the release that unlocked Owen's car seat from its base, and struggled to lift it up and out. She set the car seat down on the ground and darted her gaze toward Charley. Would he expect her to keep thinking about and making plans to help the Remarkables at a time like this?

Did she want to?

She kind of didn't want to think about anyone's death right now. She wanted to pretend to herself that people didn't die.

Charley was unbuckling his seat belt.

"Later," he mumbled, and then slid out of the minivan and ambled off into the woods. His shoulders slumped and he kept his head down, his hair falling forward to hide his face, as if he were just returning to his natural posture.

As if Marin couldn't help him or the Remarkables, and he'd known it all along.

TWENTY-SEVEN

Dad wanted to go to the funeral. A last-minute plane ticket was more than the Plucketts could afford, and it was a thirteen-hour drive, but still, Dad kept saying to Mom, "I. Have. To. Go."

Lying in bed that night, Marin could hear Mom and Dad discussing the funeral, and when she woke up at 3:00 a.m., she thought she could hear them discussing it still. It was odd—she could sleep right through Owen's middle-of-the-night, top-of-his-lungs cries every single night now. So why couldn't she tune out the low murmur of Mom's and Dad's voices talking about Uncle Pete?

"Everybody would understand if—" Mom said.

"*I* couldn't!" Dad insisted. "I couldn't forgive myself if I missed this!"

Oh. Were Mom and Dad . . . fighting?

In the morning when Marin went downstairs, Mom was sitting at the kitchen table, nursing Owen, her laptop open in front of her.

Marin glanced at the kitchen clock. Nine a.m. Marin had slept late. And usually Mom would have left for work hours ago.

"Are you off today?" Marin said hopefully.

"Working from home," Mom said, making a rueful face. "So your father can sleep."

She took a sip from a mug Dad had given her a long time ago, which looked like it was covered with Band-Aids spelling out *I Can Fix It! I'm a Nurse!* Marin sniffed. The kitchen smelled suspiciously like . . .

"You're drinking *coffee*?" Marin asked. "I thought you quit until after Owen's on solid food. Because you don't want him having caffeine."

"Desperate times, desperate measures," Mom said. "Don't tell your father." She took another sip. "Besides, it's half-decaf. So it's only half-terrible for Owen."

Mom slid her laptop to the side, and pulled out the chair beside her, for Marin to sit down.

"Listen," Mom said. "Your father and I need your help."

"Okay," Marin said, sliding into the chair.

Mom laughed.

"Now that's the attitude I like! Don't you want to know what you're agreeing to?"

"You wouldn't make me change all of Owen's diapers from now on, would you?" Marin asked, feeling proud because that was the kind of joke Dad would make.

"I wouldn't ask that of anyone," Mom said solemnly. "No, it's that . . . Dad and I have figured out a way for him to work out going to Pete's funeral. He's convinced he can make the drive in one day—one day out, and one day back, I mean. Nothing's entirely set yet, but it looks like the funeral would be on Saturday. So I would only have to work from home—or take Owen to work with me—on Friday. I think I can swing that. As Dad keeps reminding me, I'm the boss now, after all."

She wrinkled up her nose, mocking herself. Marin knew Mom thought being the boss meant she should work hardest of anyone.

"I *really* don't like the idea of your father driving thirteen hours by himself—and then turning around and doing it again, with only one day in between," Mom said. "Especially when he has nine weeks' worth of sleep debt behind him. So, what we agreed was that you would go with him, and keep him company. And keep him *awake*. Make him stop for coffee if he needs it." She lifted her coffee mug as if making a toast. "And there's something in it for you, too. You and Dad will stay at the Luskas, so you'll get to see Ashlyn, and I'll bet she'll invite Kenner over, too—maybe all three of you can have a sleepover. Remember how we said we'd make sure you could stay in touch with your friends? We just didn't expect it to happen quite so soon, for such a sad reason. . . ."

The Luskas were Ashlyn's family. Mom was saying Marin was going to see Ashlyn again. No, Marin would *have* to see Ashlyn, because how could Marin explain wanting to stay somewhere else?

All the time leaving Illinois when Mom and Dad were saying, "We'll get you back to see your friends *a lot*. We'll make it work," Marin had thought, *No, no, don't! I don't want to see them ever again! They're mean, and . . . and they made me an awful person!*

But Marin hadn't been able to say that then, and she really couldn't say it now. She felt her stomach lurch.

"Would I . . . have to go to the funeral?" she asked in a small voice. She fiddled with the place mat on the table before her.

"Only if you want to," Mom said. "I'm guessing you'll want to spend every minute you can with Ashlyn, so probably not. And that's fine."

Should she tell Mom that she and Ashlyn and Kenner weren't friends anymore? Should she tell Mom why?

Should she *confess*?

"But . . . ," she began, and stopped. Mom was rubbing her face with the hand that wasn't supporting Owen's head. For the first time, Marin noticed that Mom's eyes were red-rimmed and puffy as if she'd been crying, too, just like Dad.

Mom knew Uncle Pete, too, Marin thought. *He was her friend, too. And now I can't tell her something* else *to upset her.*

"But what?" Mom asked. Marin could see her sneaking glances back toward her laptop, where the screen kept lighting up with new email.

Marin felt even guiltier.

"But . . . if Dad's kind of . . . sad . . . and not talking much, I don't think I can talk to him for thirteen hours straight," Marin said, changing what she'd been about to say. "I don't think I can be that . . . entertaining."

Mom looked at her watch.

"How about, as soon as the library opens, we go and pick up some audiobooks for you and Dad to listen to in the car?" Mom said.

"Don't you need to work?" Marin asked.

"Oh, honey," Mom said wearily. "I've been at my computer since four a.m. I think I can take a short break."

So as soon as Marin had breakfast, brushed her teeth, and changed her clothes, they put Owen in his car seat and headed out.

"This is the first time it's been just you and me going anywhere together since Owen was born," Marin said as she fastened her seat belt. "Well, I mean, you, me, and Owen."

"Yeah, but he's not holding up his side of the conversation, is he?" Mom joked, with a glance over her shoulder as she put the car in reverse. Then she bit her lip. "Marin, I promise you, my job isn't always going to be this crazy. Neither is life with Owen. It's just because there's so much new all at once. Owen, the job . . . It was maybe a little too much to take on all at once. But I'm starting to figure out which way is up. Once I have things running a little more smoothly, I'll be able to spend more time with you. I didn't want you to think that . . . that we'd never have any more just-us time ever again."

"I know," Marin said.

"Anyhow, I know Dad's doing a great job, being more of the hands-on parent for now," Mom continued.

Somehow that made Marin feel like crying, too.

They got to the library, and Mom parked. Marin threaded her way to the *Got a Question? Ask It Here!* desk to find out where the kids' audiobooks were. The same purple-haired librarian from the day before greeted Marin like a long-lost friend.

"Ah, my young historian *amie*! That's French—I'm trying to culture up this place today," she said. "And I was hoping you'd come back! I kept thinking, after you left yesterday, didn't I *just* see something about that fire recently? You wouldn't happen to have a *Summitview Times* from a week ago last Tuesday lying around your house, would you?"

"Um, no?" Marin said. "We didn't even live in Summitview

yet a week ago last Tuesday."

"Then *bienvenue*!" the librarian exclaimed, throwing her hands up in the air. "Let this be my welcome gift to you! And justification I can give my roommates for being a pack rat and refusing to throw out old papers and magazines! Or still being old-school enough to have them around at all!"

She slid a folded-up newspaper into Marin's hand. Marin saw the headline at the top of the page: *LONG-AGO TRAGEDY INSPIRES*—

"Oh, thanks!" Marin said. She unfolded the paper to see the rest of the headline: *SMOKE DETECTOR GIVEAWAY.* "Do you need this back when I'm done with it?"

"No, no." The librarian waved away the question. "Like I said, it's a gift! A, I mean, *un . . . une?* . . . Give me a moment here . . ." She typed something quickly into her computer. "*Voilà! Un cadeau.*"

Mom finally caught up with Marin. She'd been struggling to carry Owen's car seat up the stairs—she was a lot slower with it than Dad. Marin quickly tucked the newspaper under her arm and acted like she and the librarian had been talking about audiobooks all along.

It was only later, after she'd gotten back home, that Marin sneaked the newspaper up to her room and unfolded the paper all the way, to see the whole article. She began reading:

Heather Hampton can never forget the horror she felt when she learned that her best friend in high school had just died in a house fire—and that the death could have been prevented.

"You had to know Missy Caravechio," Hampton, 37, reminisced. "She was so alive, so special. It didn't seem possible that her life would just end at seventeen. And I was there the night that . . . that . . ."

Even 20 years later, Hampton has trouble finishing that sentence. Because the tragedy that Hampton has mourned for her entire adult life was actually set in motion at a birthday party a week earlier, when a mutual friend removed the batteries from the Caravechios' smoke detector. Hampton said the friend just wanted to avoid the detector going off because of food burned on a cookie tray, even though there wasn't actually a fire.

"I saw him standing on the chair in the hallway, taking out the batteries," Hampton said. She declined to identify the mutual friend, saying, "He's been through enough already." But, she said, "All of us knew what he'd done, all of us who hung out together. And somehow none of us remembered, later that night or the next day, to say to Missy or her parents or . . . the friend . . . 'Hey, now that the party's over, how about replacing the batteries?' I still feel guilty about that."

Missy herself didn't know about the missing batteries, Ms. Hampton said, because she'd been outside helping her grandfather up the stairs into the house.

"That's the kind of person Missy was," Hampton said. "Always helping somebody."

And that's why Hampton and a small group of other friends who knew Missy started a charity in Missy's memory even before they were out of high school. They're celebrating the 20th anniversary of that charity this year. Despite separations due to college, marriages, moves, and other life events, the four women—Hampton, Lisa Bereski, Anne Stein, and Sonya Trescio—have continued to raise money for older houses to be retrofitted with smoke detectors that can run on both batteries and electricity, for people who wouldn't be able to afford the change themselves.

"It just seems so much safer if the detectors work two ways," Hampton said. "With the smoke detectors hardwired in, they could go off even if there weren't batteries. But the batteries can be backup for if a fire occurs when the electricity is out."

By the group's calculation, they've given away 500 smoke detectors in the past 20 years. Although they haven't been able to check back with every single home they've made safer—"Are you kidding?" Hampton asked. "When all four of us have kids and jobs on top of this charity?"—Hampton knows of three situations where the improved detectors did indeed send residents to safety during a fire.

"We can't really take too much credit," Hampton said, "because we don't know if those families would have escaped regardless. But even if we're just giving out peace of mind, that's enough. I know it's what Missy would have wanted us to do."

One happy result of the charity is indisputable: Hampton met her husband, Steve, because of it. Steve Hampton, an electrician, volunteered to help install some of the donated smoke detectors 15 years ago, and, well, let's just say sparks flew. . . .

The rest of the story was about a fund-raiser planned for the women's charity. Marin lowered the newspaper. A picture at the bottom of the story showed four women holding a framed portrait of a teenager. The picture was too small and grainy to make out much about either the women or the teenager, but two of the women looked vaguely familiar.

Because I saw them as they looked twenty years ago, as Remarkables? Marin wondered. *Or . . .*

Marin checked the names under the picture. The two women who looked familiar were Heather Hampton and Lisa Bereski. Heather and Lisa. Why did those names sound familiar, too?

Then Marin knew. They were two of the mothers Marin had met in the crying room at the church. The third woman in the crying room, Oliver's mom, had said that Heather and Lisa had been friends since preschool.

Marin felt tingly all over. Was everyone connected in a town as small as Summitview? It felt like more than a coincidence, that two of the very few adults Marin had met in Summitview were connected to Missy Caravechio and Charley's dad.

Marin went back and reread the paragraph about how Heather Hampton had seen Charley's dad take out the smoke detector batteries—because of course she meant Charley's dad. Marin read the sentence *I still feel guilty about that* three times.

Charley's dad felt guilty, and he'd started using drugs, and at least according to Charley, that guilt had destroyed his life. He hadn't even seen his own children in five years.

Heather Hampton felt guilty, and she'd started a charity that helped hundreds of people, and had maybe even saved people's lives.

Was the difference just that Charley's dad felt more responsible, because he'd been the person who actually removed the batteries?

Oh, Marin thought, jerking upright. *If we go back and save Missy Caravechio's life, which ends the guilt for Charley's dad and maybe fixes his life, we'll also stop Heather*

Hampton's guilt. So she wouldn't start her charity.

And maybe some of the people she'd helped might even die.

Marin had to talk to Charley about all of this.

She snatched up the paper and raced out of her bedroom and down the stairs.

"I'm going outside!" she yelled to Mom and Dad as soon as she got to the back door. She didn't even wait to hear if either one of them called back.

But when she got to Charley's clubhouse, he was nowhere in sight.

"Charley not having a cell phone is *crazy*," she griped to herself.

It would be easier for Marin to get in touch with Ashlyn or Kenner than Charley right now, and they were three states away.

Not that I want to get in touch with Ashlyn or Kenner, Marin thought. *Except now I'll have to see them again, I'll have to talk to them, and Dad will find out everything. . . .*

Hot shame flooded her gut.

She forced herself to go back to thinking about Charley and the Remarkables.

"Charley? Charley?" she called. She put the newspaper down on the table and poked her head out the clubhouse door, shouting out into the trees.

No one answered.

What if Marin didn't see Charley again before she had to leave for Illinois with Dad? And what if Charley figured everything out and tried to change the past while she was away? He needed to see this article so he'd know it was all more complicated than they'd thought. Saving Missy Caravechio's life wasn't enough; somehow Charley and Marin needed to make sure Missy lived *and* Heather still started her charity anyway.

Marin hunted around on the ground until she found a large rock. She put it down on the newspaper to hold it in place, for Charley to see the next time he came back to the clubhouse.

Then she noticed the lock was gone from the drawer and the table leg. She pulled out the drawer, and found a sheet of blank paper and a blue colored pencil.

Dear Charley, she wrote. *I have to go back to Illinois with my dad for a few days. I thought you should see this. The librarian gave it to me.*

Her head swam a little, thinking of all the connections she'd figured out, all the complications. It would take a really, really long letter to explain everything. Charley would probably understand just from reading the article, anyhow. She decided only to sum up what mattered most:

We can still fix everything. I promise!

She looked at the last word, and knew it wasn't quite right. She couldn't actually promise anything. She just wanted to believe it was that certain, and wanted Charley to believe, too.

If it was possible for them to see time travelers, wasn't everything else they wanted possible, too? With the Remarkables, anyway . . .

Marin didn't change anything she'd written. She added her name, slid the note under the rock with the newspaper, and walked away.

TWENTY-EIGHT

Dad and Marin had just crossed the border from Indiana into Illinois when Marin pulled out her phone.

"I'll let Ashlyn know we're an hour away," she told Dad.

"Yep," Dad said, which was totally un-Dad-like. In her head, Marin could hear what Dad should have said: *Oh, yeah! Tell her to tell her parents we're flying like the wind! We're making great time! Totally legal and staying within the posted speed limit at all times, of course! And I'm fresh as a daisy even after getting up at four and driving twelve hours. What was your mom so worried about?*

Because Dad *didn't* say that, it was impossible for Marin to tell him how things actually were between her and Ashlyn. So she had to get a warning to Ashlyn. All through Pennsylvania and Ohio and Indiana, she'd tried to work out what she could say in this text, even as the landscape around her smoothed out from mountains and forests to flat fields of soybeans and corn. Still, her thumbs hesitated over her phone screen. Finally she wrote: **My dad doesn't know we aren't friends anymore. He's already upset because of his friend dying. I don't want to upset him worse. So could you please just pretend?**

The area of the phone screen below Marin's text stayed empty and blank. After a moment, Marin added: **I mean, you just have to pretend while we're around my dad. You don't have to talk to me otherwise if you don't want to.**

Still nothing. Marin imagined Ashlyn and Kenner giggling together over her text, their heads bent so close together that their light brown and blond hair blended together, just a shadow's difference between them. Ashlyn was probably that very moment laughing into Kenner's ear, *Marin actually thinks I'd do anything to help her or her family? After what she said to us? She's crazy! I'm going to embarrass her so bad!* And Kenner would say, *Yeah, give her what she deserves....*

Marin's stomach churned. It felt like the french fries she'd eaten with her McDonald's lunch had turned into swords, and they were all stabbing her.

Fifteen minutes later, Marin's phone dinged, and Marin jumped.

"Are they preparing the red carpet to welcome us back into town?" Dad asked, which would have been reassuring if he hadn't said it in such a sad voice.

Marin looked at her phone. Ashlyn had written back, **My**

parents don't know we're not friends anymore either. So you pretend, too.

What?

The french fries in Marin's stomach seemed to turn back into regular, half-digested french fries.

"Well?" Dad said.

"I . . . I guess they're ready for us," Marin said.

When they finally pulled up in front of Ashlyn's house, Marin felt a jolt of something like electricity, because everything was so familiar. It had only been three weeks since the last time she'd been at Ashlyn's house, but everything had changed for Marin since then. So it seemed weird that the rosebushes in front of the Luskas' house weren't any taller than they'd been before. And the front door still had the little dent right beside the doorknob, where Marin herself had hit it with a softball (but only because Ashlyn didn't catch the ball, because she said Marin threw too hard). And Marin still had every single bumper sticker on Mrs. Luska's car memorized, from *MY CHILD IS AN HONOR ROLL STUDENT AT ALCOTT ELEMENTARY* to *I SELL MARY KAY* to *MY OTHER CAR IS A GOLF CART*. (None of the Luskas had ever played golf. It was just too hard to take off that old bumper sticker when they bought the car.) The car sat in the carport, just like always, resting against the tennis balls Mr. Luska had hung to mark the right place to stop, and Marin could remember Ashlyn complaining to her dad, "Why don't we have a garage like other people?" and Mr. Luska had said, "Because we're tough enough to take stepping outside even in the wintertime in Illinois, and don't you forget it." Marin glanced up at the window of Ashlyn's room, and the glare from the sun made it impossible to see in. But Marin could remember how excited Ashlyn had been when she'd gotten Disney Princess curtains, and then when Ashlyn had decided those curtains were babyish, and she'd talked her mom into replacing them with tie-dye hot pink and neon green.

So many memories. It felt like half of Marin's life had taken place at the Luskas'.

It felt so weird to be back in a place where everything was familiar, not new and strange.

Marin and Dad got out of the car. Marin started to reach for her duffel bag on the back seat, but Dad said, "Oh, go see your friend. We can get that later."

And then Marin had to walk up the front steps and knock on the door.

Ashlyn opened the door.

Ashlyn looked totally familiar, too. It looked like she'd straightened her wavy, light brown hair, something she'd started doing only in fifth grade, but Marin could tell that the one lock a quarter of the way back on the left side still rebelled, as always; trying to straighten it had only made it stick out more. Marin could picture the exact rack at Claire's where Ashlyn had gotten her little gold hoop earrings; Marin had been with Ashlyn and Ashlyn's mom last summer when they'd bought her purple top with the cutout sleeves and her jeans shorts with the glitter along the hem. The three of them had been shopping at Justice, and Ashlyn had spent forever in the changing room, deciding, so Marin and Ashlyn's mom had spent part of the time looking at cute dog pictures on Mrs. Luska's phone.

Also: Ashlyn's knees didn't have scabs on them anymore, like they always did when Marin and Ashlyn were little, but in one glance Marin could remember the source of every little scar on Ashlyn's legs. One was from when she was learning how to Rollerblade; one was from the first time Ashlyn's dad took the training wheels off Ashlyn's bike. One was from when Marin and Ashlyn had taken that acting class together, and Ashlyn had tripped on the stairs up to the stage. . . .

I hope Ashlyn and I actually learned something in that acting class besides how to pretend to be trees, Marin thought, and only then did she dare to look Ashlyn in the eye.

She kind of wanted to make a joke to Ashlyn about pretending to be a tree, and it made her sad that they couldn't joke like that anymore.

And . . . she kind of wanted Ashlyn to see that she was sad. That she was sad and . . . still mad and . . .

And sorry, Marin thought. *What if I just tell Ashlyn I'm sorry?*

But Ashlyn was reaching out to pull Marin into a hug, and Marin could feel how fake the hug was, Ashlyn patting Marin on the back even as she used her elbows to keep Marin from getting too close.

That wasn't how Ashlyn gave hugs. Ashlyn hugged people *tight*, usually while squealing and jumping up and down.

Ashlyn let go, so Marin did, too.

And then Mrs. Luska was there, hugging Marin like she always did, and Mr. Luska was shouting from the back of the house, "Plucketts, hello!" And then Dad stumbled into the house behind Marin, and the Luskas were hugging him and telling him how sorry they were about Uncle Pete.

Marin and Ashlyn stood off to the side just looking at each other. Ashlyn's mouth was pressed into a thin, disapproving line, and her eyes were hard and emotionless, like a pair of marbles.

Marin felt someone nudge her shoulder.

"Oh, go on, you two," Dad said. "You do not need to stand there being all quiet and serious for the sake of us sad grown-ups. You have thirty-six hours together, and I'm sorry it's not more, but—go! Make the best of it!"

"Want to come up to my room?" Ashlyn said carefully, as if she were reading lines in a play.

"Sure," Marin said. Did anyone notice how fake her voice sounded, too?

They climbed the stairs, and in the doorway to Ashlyn's room, Marin saw that everything here was different. The walls were turquoise now, not pink, and the bedspread had black and white zigzags.

"Nice," Marin said, stepping in, even though she really wanted to say, *There was nothing wrong with the way it used to be!* The room now looked more like a picture on the internet, or a display in a store, rather than a bedroom a real person lived in. A bedroom that *Ashlyn* lived in. The room even smelled like paint instead of the mix of spearmint gum and shampoo and, well, *glitter* that Marin associated with Ashlyn.

Marin couldn't even have described what glitter smelled like, except to say, *Ashlyn*.

"Do you have any pictures on your phone of what your new room looks like?" Ashlyn asked stiffly, as if Marin were a stranger she'd just met. Ashlyn nudged the door shut behind them, and maybe Marin should just be glad that Ashlyn was still talking to her at all, now that they were away from the parents and didn't have to pretend anymore.

"My room's not really done yet," Marin said, because she wasn't going to say that she was still using the same old faded blue-jeans-like bedspread and red pillows she'd had in Illinois, and she didn't care. "My books are in stacks all over the place, because Dad says he's going to build new bookshelves for me, but he hasn't had a chance to do that yet. And I need his help putting up pictures and posters on the wall, and the only time he has is when Owen is sleeping, but my room is right next to Owen's and we don't want to wake him up hammering the walls. . . ."

"Ooh, Owen!" Ashlyn squealed, practically sounding like herself again. "Do you have pictures of *him* on your phone? I bet he's grown so much!"

Of course Marin had those. She handed over her phone. Both girls sat down on the bed, leaning together so Marin could narrate. As Ashlyn swiped through the photos, oohing and aahing, Marin started feeling like maybe everything was going to be okay. Ashlyn and Marin had apparently learned enough in that one acting class that they could pretend perfectly well for the next thirty-six hours. Even when they were alone in a room together, they could still pretend.

"He's so adorable," Ashlyn said wistfully, and Marin remembered how excited Ashlyn had been all those months ago when Marin had told her, "Guess what? My mom's pregnant!" And way back then, Marin had said, "I promise, I'll share, so it'll almost be like *you* have a new baby in your family, too."

Marin hadn't known then that her family was going to

move. Nobody had known. So Marin hadn't known then that she would have to break her promise.

But it would never be like Owen was Ashlyn's little brother, too. Owen wouldn't remember the few weeks he'd lived in Illinois. He wouldn't grow up even knowing who Ashlyn was.

Marin wanted to give something back to Ashlyn to make up for the broken promise, so she said, "Just think how adorable these pictures would be if you were the one who took them!"

Ashlyn *was* great at pictures. She was good enough to be a professional photographer when she grew up. Maybe she was that good already. She had the best Instagram account of anyone Marin knew—though Marin hadn't looked at it in three weeks—and Ashlyn's parents were really nice about letting Ashlyn print out the pictures she liked best, as big as she wanted, and hang them all over her room.

That was what made this room seem so empty and wrong for Ashlyn—it had absolutely nothing hanging on the walls.

"I guess you just have all your pictures down from when you were painting, huh?" Marin said, glancing around for some huge stack of prints.

She was sitting close enough to Ashlyn to feel how Ashlyn's posture suddenly went rigid.

And then Marin remembered that virtually every single picture that had been up on Ashlyn's wall had included Marin: Ashlyn's selfies of the two of them eating ice cream cones together or going trick-or-treating together or playing with makeup together, or just solo photos of Marin rolling her eyes and sticking out her tongue at Ashlyn, or grinning as wide as she could at Ashlyn, or holding up a picture of the two of them as toddlers and making a face as if to say, *Who dressed us like that back then?*

"I mean, your *newest* pictures," Marin said quickly, trying to cover for her mistake. "The ones from the last few weeks! With, um, Kenner!"

Her voice came out panicked, not calm, but she felt proud that she could even speak Kenner's name to Ashlyn.

To Marin's surprise, Ashlyn buried her face in Marin's shoulder. It happened so fast, Marin didn't even see her move.

"Don't you know Kenner and I aren't friends anymore, *either*?" Ashlyn wailed, her face twisted against Marin's sleeve.

Was she crying? Really crying?

Marin felt a tear roll down onto her arm.

Marin lifted a hand to pat Ashlyn's shoulder, and she opened her mouth to say, *No! I'm sorry! I didn't know! What happened?* But just then Ashlyn gave her such a hard shove that Marin almost fell off the bed.

"And don't you know it's all your fault?" Ashlyn asked.

TWENTY-NINE

"What are you talking about?" Marin asked. "I haven't even been here!"

"That last night you were!" Ashlyn accused. "When you said . . ."

And maybe Charley was right, and time travel actually existed. Because suddenly everything came back like it was happening all over again, everything Marin had tried to avoid thinking about for the past three weeks. She looked down, and it was like she wasn't seeing the jagged black and white of Ashlyn's current bedspread, but the irregular blotches of Ashlyn's old tie-dye.

It had been the night of her last sleepover with Ashlyn and Kenner, and they'd just gotten back from Marin's last trip to Mudlow's for ice cream, the last time she'd have to hear Kenner complain, *That is the stupidest name for an ice cream place! Who would ever want to eat "All your favorite flavors of mud"?* And it was also the last time Marin had countered, *I would! Mudlow's is the best!* Nothing had felt right to Marin that night. She was getting tired of lasts, and she found herself wondering if she could get away with saying, *You know what? I'm really tired. Why don't we just go to sleep?* But probably if she did that, Kenner and Ashlyn would stay awake and draw a mustache on her face with a black Sharpie as soon as she was asleep, or draw circles and fake eyelashes around her eyes.

After all, they'd done that before.

And then the three girls had walked into Ashlyn's bedroom, the sweet aftertaste of the ice cream already feeling wrong in Marin's mouth. And Kenner had said, "Ashlyn, why do you still have that ugly bedspread? It looks like puddles of dog vomit!"

And Marin had snapped, "Why do you have to be so mean?"

Then Ashlyn had taken a step forward, hovering right between Marin and Kenner. Marin had expected Ashlyn to step over beside her and say something like, *Yeah, Kenner. If you're going to be mean, you should just go home, so you don't ruin Marin's last night.*

Instead, Ashlyn had stepped toward Kenner, and said in a weak, shaky voice, "Marin, stop it. Kenner's just trying to help. So we'll be ready for middle school."

Something had exploded inside Marin then. Everything she'd bottled up inside all spring long—every barb and jab and taunt and whisper she thought she'd managed to ignore and get past—maybe none of it had rolled off her the way she thought. Apparently she'd been keeping score in a way she hadn't even noticed, and every cruelty Marin had endured had actually gotten under her skin and festered and grown and sparked a fury that Marin couldn't control.

She'd never felt like this before in her life.

"I hate you both!" she'd snarled back at Ashlyn and Kenner. "You're terrible people! You're so mean I won't miss either of you at all—I'm *glad* I'm getting away from you! I hope you both *fail* in middle school, and nobody likes you, and they laugh at everything you wear, and you get kicked out of every club you join, and, oh, yeah, there is no way either one of you could ever be a cheerleader! Ashlyn couldn't do a cartwheel if her life depended on it! And you, Kenner—you'll never be able to do the splits!"

The *I hope you both fail* was particularly mean to Ashlyn, because she tried so hard to get good grades. But it was true that she wasn't good at cartwheels, either.

Kenner just kept glaring back at Marin, as if she'd been wearing armor to protect her against every single one of Marin's words. But Ashlyn absolutely wilted, like a flower shriveling up and dying right before Marin's eyes. She reeled backward, like she was about to faint. She might have even fallen to the floor if Kenner hadn't wrapped her arms around her, holding her up.

Marin spun on her heel and ran to Ashlyn's bathroom to throw up every bit of the Mudlow's ice cream in her stomach.

For a long time, she stayed in the bathroom, pressing her hot face against the cold porcelain of the toilet bowl. She cried, and then she stopped crying, and then she cried again, and neither Ashlyn nor Kenner knocked on the door to say, *Are you all right?* Or *Do you need us to call your mom and dad?*

Finally Marin stood up and ran water over her face. She brushed her teeth—she'd stayed over at Ashlyn's so many times that she had her own toothbrush standing in the same toothbrush holder with Ashlyn's.

Probably the Luskas would just throw away Marin's toothbrush now, and replace it with one for Kenner.

Probably they *should,* because that toothbrush would never again taste like anything but vomit.

Marin looked at herself in the mirror, and it was like looking at a total stranger. People always said that Marin had such kind eyes, such a beautiful hazel color like her mom's, but those eyes were just flat and lifeless now, like an ugly doll's. It was true, as Kenner often accused her, that Marin didn't care very much about combing or brushing her hair all the time, but Marin was lucky because her hair was dark and thick and straight all on its own, so usually it looked perfectly tidy without Marin having to try very hard. But now it stuck out all over the place, as if someone had tied knots or brambles into it. And Marin's skin was blotchy from crying; her nose was crusty with a combination of tears and snot—how could her body crank out so many disgusting substances all at once?

I look, Marin thought, *exactly like someone who could tell her two best friends* I hate you! *on the very last night we're ever going to spend together.*

Marin had never said the words *I hate you* to anyone before.

Marin stepped out of the bathroom before she could start crying again.

Ashlyn and Kenner were lying on the floor in their sleeping bags, both of them staring at their phones.

If either one of them had shot her a sympathetic look or whispered *I'm sorry*—or done anything at all to indicate that they cared that Marin existed—Marin would have broken down and hugged them both and burbled out, *I'm sorry! I'm so, so sorry! I didn't mean any of it! I'm just so sad that I'm leaving you, and that's why I said that, and, oh, you know I'll be your friend forever! You know that, don't you?*

But neither of them so much as blinked in Marin's direction. They just kept staring at their phones.

Marin kept her heart hard and stepped past them to pick up her own sleeping bag and pillow and backpack. And she kept her voice perfectly emotionless as she said, "I'm going to sleep in the guest bedroom. *Don't* bother me."

And she went into the Luskas' guest room, and even though she prayed, "Please let someone come, and I'll apologize. Please," nobody came for her.

Marin cried herself to sleep.

In the morning, she woke up early, still crying, but something like ice had grown around her heart—or maybe it was more like the invisible armor Kenner had found for herself the night before.

With great precision, Marin had texted her parents: Can you come get me now? The Luskas had something come up. Then she rolled up her sleeping bag and wrapped the cord around it before tucking her pillow inside. She realized she'd slept in her clothes—*easier that way,* she told herself—and so she just shouldered her backpack and picked up her sleeping bag roll, and tiptoed downstairs.

She'd hoped she was early enough that Ashlyn's parents wouldn't even be awake, but Mrs. Luska was hunched over a laptop in the family room. She took one look at Marin, and rushed over and gave her a big hug with the words "Oh, honey. Moving is hard, isn't it?"

Marin opened her mouth, and for a moment it was touch and go whether she would spill everything. Mrs. Luska was almost like Marin's second mother. She'd known Marin practically since she was born.

But then Mrs. Luska said, "This is what I think it's going

to feel like when Ashlyn goes off to college. It's like you're my own kid, leaving me," and that was enough to remind Marin that Mrs. Luska belonged to Ashlyn. Marin was only *like* Mrs. Luska's own kid; Ashlyn actually *was* hers. There was no way Marin could tell Mrs. Luska what she'd said to Ashlyn, how badly she'd hurt her.

It would just make Mrs. Luska hate Marin, too.

And then Dad had pulled into the driveway, and Marin had thought, *That's it. I'll never see Ashlyn or Kenner again.*

But here Marin was, back in Ashlyn's room. And Ashlyn was accusing Marin of ruining her friendship with Kenner, too.

"Looked to me like you and Kenner were on the same side that night," Marin said. And somehow, even though the words felt bitter and brittle and cutting in Marin's head, they came out just sounding sad. Marin waited for the same rush of fury she'd felt the last time, but it didn't arrive.

Ashlyn burst into tears again.

"I thought I had to side with Kenner!" she wailed, angrily rubbing her hands across her face, to wipe away her tears. "Because you were leaving! If I lost you and then I lost Kenner, too, then . . . then . . . who would I have? I'd have to start middle school alone! And now . . ." She sniffed. "Now I really am going to start middle school alone! Because Kenner says I'm boring, and she started hanging out with Caitlyn Russo and Deirdre Spann, and—and . . ."

"That Kenner is just so mean!" Marin exploded. Oh, yes. The anger was still there, after all. "Why were we ever friends with her?"

The *we* just slipped out. Like there was a *we* again.

Ashlyn's whole face quivered, so much like Owen's when he was about to let out his most heartbroken sob. Nine weeks of having a baby brother had made Marin an expert on the stages of crying. It wasn't so different between babies and eleven-year-olds.

Marin thought about how much she'd seen her dad cry in the past few days. Maybe it wasn't even that different between babies and adults.

"Sometimes Kenner could be fun," Ashlyn said forlornly. "And nice." She gulped. "Nice to *me*, anyway. Most of the time. She always told me not to tell you, but *I* was really her best friend, her favorite person in the world. And I knew you thought I was your best friend, too. And that made me feel so—so . . . like some kind of a treasure. You know? You're always better at school than I am, and you're a *lot* better at sports. But this made me feel like *I* was the one that everyone liked best." She sniffed, her face trembly again. "Even if it was just you and Kenner."

There were so many things Marin could have yelled back at Ashlyn. *Just me and Kenner?* "*Just*"? *When it had always been you and me, and* we'd *been best friends since we could walk? Why didn't you ever stick up for me against Kenner? Why didn't you say, "I already have a best friend, thank you very much! Now—go away!"*

But Marin didn't actually feel like shouting. Not when she could feel her face going all Owen-quivery, too. Not when she had a cruel voice whispering in her head, *Kenner never told me not to tell Ashlyn that I was actually Kenner's best friend. Kenner must have just been pretending to like me to get to Ashlyn.*

Why did Marin even care if Kenner liked her? Why care about someone liking you when you didn't like them?

Ashlyn buried her face in her hands.

"And now you hate me, and I *deserve* to have you hate me, because Kenner and I *were* awful to you, and—"

"I don't hate you," Marin said. She sighed. "I never hated you. I was just mad that night, and I felt weird about moving and . . . and maybe I did know that Kenner liked you better, and I was jealous, and . . . I'm sorry. We're still friends. Even if you don't want to be friends with me, I'm still friends with you."

Marin could feel tears streaming down her cheeks, and Ashlyn's face was a snotty, tearstained mess. But it didn't feel like they were still crying for the same reasons. Now Marin's tears felt more like a relief.

She didn't feel guilty anymore. The feeling she'd carried

for the past three weeks—that she was a terrible person; that no matter what she did, she could never make up for it—was gone.

"But . . . but . . . you still moved to Pa-Pa-Pennsylvania," Ashlyn sobbed. "I still don't have any friends *here*! I'm still going to start middle school alone!"

Marin reached over to Ashlyn's nightstand. She pulled out a Kleenex and handed it to Ashlyn. Then she playfully bumped her shoulder into Ashlyn's.

"Hey," Marin said. "I'm in the same boat. We'll be alone, well . . . sort of together. I'm going off to middle school alone, too. And I won't know *anyone*. At least you'll *know* everyone from our elementary school, even if they aren't friends. Yet."

Ashlyn blew her nose feebly into the Kleenex.

"But you don't really *need* friends the way I do," Ashlyn said. "You're fine just reading a book or playing a game on your phone or bouncing a basketball. . . . You can be by yourself, no problem. I can't."

Was that true?

Marin thought about her first day in the new house in Pennsylvania, when she'd explored the woods by herself. Ashlyn, she knew, wouldn't have done that. She would have begged one of her parents to go with her, or just waited until she finally found a friend.

Ashlyn would never have found the Remarkables. She would have been right there, her backyard touching theirs, and never known it.

She wouldn't have been brave enough to go looking for Charley all by herself, either.

"It's, like, that night when you told off Kenner and me—and you were right! You were so right! Kenner was being mean!—you could just walk away," Ashlyn said. "Kenner and me, we started arguing after you went into the bathroom, and Kenner was even meaner to me, and I couldn't fight back. And then you came out of the bathroom, and you said, 'I'm going to the guest room. Don't bother me,' and you were so dignified. It was like you were grown-up or something. In charge. And I couldn't do anything but lie there staring at my phone, because I was so afraid that if I said anything nice to you, Kenner would stop being my friend. And then she stopped being my friend anyhow! I thought we'd all make up in the morning, but you were already gone, and it was like you didn't care anymore. . . ."

"I didn't *feel* dignified," Marin said. "Or in charge. Not once that night. Couldn't you hear how much I cried?"

But maybe Ashlyn hadn't. Now Marin remembered putting her hand over her mouth as she sobbed, so no one would hear her. Her crying that night hadn't been Owen-like. She'd done it as silently and secretly as she could.

And she *had* walked away. Because she was moving, regardless.

Marin put her arm around Ashlyn's shoulders.

"We both messed up," she said. "But, really, Ashlyn, you've got to learn how to deal with bullies before you start middle school."

It was the first time she'd used the word *bully* to herself about Kenner. But it fit.

"I never had to before," Ashlyn sobbed, putting her face down on Marin's shoulder. "You always did it for me! Even when it was just Kenner saying stupid stuff about my bedspread!"

Marin reached for her phone with the hand that wasn't holding on to Ashlyn.

"When's your first day of school?" she asked.

"August . . . August fourteenth," Ashlyn sniffled.

Marin wrote that down one-handedly in her phone.

"Okay," Marin said. "School in Pennsylvania doesn't start until later—it's the day after Labor Day, I think. So on August fourteenth, I will text you every hour, starting when you get up, and it'll be stuff like, 'You can do this!' and 'You have a friend! Pretend I'm there with you and stay away from bullies!' And maybe, 'Look around for the new kids! They need new friends as much as you do! Be kind to the ones who need it most!'"

Ashlyn giggled through her tears.

"Now you sound like your dad," she said. "Remember how in gym class, he'd say, 'Be kind. That's the first rule,' like, a hundred times a day?"

"I won't say it a hundred times," Marin said. "Dad talks a lot more than I do." She looked down at her hands. "And . . . that's why I'm scared about starting at a new school and not knowing anyone. Who notices a new kid who's really quiet?"

"So *I'll* text *you* on your first day of school," Ashlyn said. "I'll tell you . . . I don't know, maybe, 'Look around for the *other* quiet new kids.'" She wasn't crying anymore. And now she patted Marin's back. It had suddenly changed, who was comforting whom. "Have you met any other kids in Pennsylvania yet?"

"There's a boy my age who lives right next door," Marin said. "But he goes to a different school."

Ashlyn raised an eyebrow and tilted her head to the side. Then she started waggling both eyebrows up and down.

"Is he cute?" she asked. "Maybe even cute enough that you'd want to talk your parents into letting you go to his school?"

Marin should have known that Ashlyn would want to know what Charley looked like. She thought about how she'd first seen him: running away, just a blur of dark hair and movement.

"I guess he's cute, but . . . it's not like that," Marin said.

She tried to think how to explain Charley to Ashlyn. It felt like she had to protect him. "He's got . . . secrets."

"Ooooh," Ashlyn said. Now she was raising and lowering her voice. "The mysterious boy next door! I like!"

How could Marin feel like she and Ashlyn had completely made up a moment ago, and yet now it seemed like Ashlyn couldn't understand her at all?

It almost felt like, even though Marin had known Ashlyn her whole life, she had more in common with Charley now.

THIRTY

Dad and Marin drove away from Ashlyn's house at 5:00 a.m. Sunday morning. They'd told the Luskas not to bother getting up to see them off, but all three of them still did.

Marin's last glimpse of Ashlyn was Ashlyn standing on her front porch waving and waving and waving. And in between waves, she waggled her thumbs in the air to pantomime texting.

As soon as they were out of sight, Marin texted Ashlyn, I know! August 14! I'll remember!

And Ashlyn texted back, And I'll remember Sept. 3! And . . . we'll text lots of other times, too, right?

Right.

Ok, now I'm going back to bed, Ashlyn wrote.

Marin slipped her phone back into her backpack and sighed.

"I know, it's hard saying goodbye *again*," Dad said, turning out of Ashlyn's neighborhood. "But you had fun, didn't you? What all did you and Ashlyn do?" Dad had stayed so late visiting with Uncle Pete's family after the funeral that he and

Marin really hadn't had a chance to talk the night before. "Did you go to Mudlow's?"

"No, we didn't really feel like ice cream," Marin said. *Not after the last time,* she added silently in her head.

"Did you go to Kenner's, or did she come over to Ashlyn's? Or did you meet somewhere like the pool?"

"We didn't see Kenner," Marin said carefully. "She and Ashlyn aren't friends anymore."

Dad hit the brakes so hard that Marin jolted forward and then back. He jerked his gaze toward the clock on the dashboard screen, which now read 5:05.

"Okay, it is way too early for you to go over and see Kenner now, but we could go park somewhere and sleep in the car for a few hours, and then you could have *some* time with Kenner," Dad said. "As long as we leave by noon, we could still be home by . . . let's see . . ."

"Dad, what are you even talking about?" Marin asked. She rubbed her neck. Was this how people got whiplash?

"It's ridiculous for you to be so close by and not see Kenner," Dad said. "And maybe it would be good for her if . . ."

Marin's stomach gurgled just at the thought of seeing Kenner.

"Dad, Kenner and I aren't friends anymore, either," Marin said. "She was mean to me and Ashlyn. Like, a *bully*. It's *good* we aren't friends anymore."

Could Marin say that now only because it was so early in the morning, and still dark in the car—and because there was no other way to stop Dad from forcing her to see Kenner?

Or could she say it only because she and Ashlyn had made up?

It felt a little like she was tattling, and a little like she was confessing.

But mostly it just felt like she was telling the truth.

"Oh, Marin," Dad said quietly. "Do you want to tell me more about—"

"No," Marin said, the word jumping out before she had time to think.

Dad went back to driving, and didn't say anything else right away. But he reached over and squeezed Marin's knee, and that made it okay not to have a lot of words between them.

They were on the highway access road where there weren't any stoplights before Dad added, "I feel like I should have seen it, I should have asked more questions. . . . Sometimes it was such a tightrope act, being a teacher at your school and being your dad. . . ."

"Dad, you shouldn't have asked *me* more questions!" Marin protested.

This time Dad laughed and ruffled her hair. But he got serious again right away.

"Then I'll tell you something. . . . I think this is okay to say now. Evidently Mrs. Luska knew some of this, so I'm not violating confidentiality. . . . I did know Kenner was having a rough time last school year. All the teachers knew."

It was on the tip of Marin's tongue to say, *Well, yeah. She was mean all the time! That is rough!* But the teachers wouldn't have seen or heard that. Kenner made her cruelest comments when adults weren't around.

So Marin asked instead, "Dad, what do you mean?"

Dad kept his eyes directed straight ahead, staring out the windshield.

"Her parents were having problems—fighting a lot—so when Kenner started having stomachaches last fall, they thought it was just stress. But then her parents were doing better, and Kenner was still sick, so they took her for medical tests. . . . For a long time, there weren't any answers, and the possibilities kept getting scarier. Cancer was one of the things they tested for."

"Kenner has cancer?" Marin reeled back, almost as if Dad had hit the brakes again.

"*No,*" Dad said. "Thank God, no. Nothing like that. I guess there were some false-positive tests along the way—and some doctors who told her she was imagining the whole thing—but Kenner doesn't have anything life-threatening. She just has some food allergies that weren't showing up in the usual ways. The worst problem is that she can't have ice cream anymore, not the real stuff, but, you know, there are lots of other choices out there now. . . ."

Mudlow's, Marin thought. That last night they'd been together, besides complaining about how much she hated Mudlow's, Kenner had also made a big deal about how ice cream cones were for babies, and *she* just wanted a little bag of organic pretzels.

Why hadn't Kenner just said she couldn't eat ice cream, instead of acting like there was something wrong with Marin and Ashlyn for liking it?

"But, Dad, Kenner didn't tell me—or Ashlyn—any of that!" Marin protested. She thought about how Ashlyn had talked about Kenner—there was no way she'd known. Also, Ashlyn wasn't great at keeping secrets; her face always gave her away. "Why didn't Kenner tell us? We could have helped! Mom could have given advice about the medical stuff, and—"

"Marin, I'm really walking a line here, because there are things I know only from meetings at school." Dad rubbed his bald head like he was buffing it. "I don't want to violate anyone's privacy. But you know Kenner. And . . . you know her parents. Maybe you can figure out some of Kenner's reasons."

Kenner's mom was really pretty, and her dad was tall and

handsome—and that was about all Marin knew. Kenner's parents weren't friendly like the Luskas. Kenner had bragged once, "My parents treat me like a grown-up. They don't mess in my business all the time, like *yours* do." Had that actually been bragging, or making excuses? There'd been another time last fall when Marin had studied really hard for a math test, and then she'd been so proud to get a perfect score. But Kenner had ruined it, because she'd seen Marin's paper and said very loudly, "You know teachers are just nice to you because they're friends with your dad. This school isn't fair at all. My dad's a lawyer, and he's going to come to school and make them treat me right. . . ."

Marin gasped. She *had* seen some of what was going on with Kenner. She just hadn't understood.

"Did Kenner's parents blame the *school* for making her sick?" Marin asked. "Did they have lots and lots of meetings—and then always take Kenner out for a special lunch afterward?"

Dad pressed his lips into a thin line. But the corners twitched.

"You said it, I didn't," he muttered.

All those times Kenner had made fun of their teachers—was it because Kenner was getting bad grades? All those times Kenner went on and on about what was and wasn't normal—was it because she was afraid she might have something terribly wrong with *her*?

"I wish I'd known," Marin said, even though this was making her feel a little sorry for Kenner, and she didn't actually want that. Not now, not when she'd just started feeling good about teaming up with Ashlyn against their ex-friend.

Why was everything so complicated?

"Yeah . . . ," Dad said. "I think I can also tell you that whenever we teachers were trying to figure out what to do about Kenner—and, well, her parents, too—there was always a moment when someone would say, 'But Kenner's friends with Marin Pluckett, and we all know Marin's a good influence, so that's got to be helping.' And I was always so proud, that that was how the other teachers saw you. My daughter, the good influence! I never thought about *you* having problems with Kenner, too. Even . . . her bullying you? How did we miss that? Did—"

"Everything's okay now," Marin said, because she still didn't want to drag out every little detail. But then she admitted, "I could have told. Or . . . asked for help."

Somehow that seemed true now, though it hadn't seemed true last spring.

Dad reached the ramp for the highway. He hit the gas and pulled onto it, the early morning road completely open before them. It felt good to be moving faster now, when they had so many miles to go. Marin would miss Ashlyn, but it felt like she was escaping from Kenner all over again.

Was it wrong to still dislike Kenner, if she'd only been mean because she was having problems?

That made Marin think of Charley's dad, who messed up his life after Missy Caravechio died.

And Charley, who could get so prickly talking about his parents.

"Dad, are the only nice people in the world just nice because they haven't had any really bad things happen to them?" Marin asked.

Dad had just started to take a sip of coffee from his travel mug, and he coughed and almost spit it out.

"Whatever gave you that idea?" Dad asked.

"Well, you and Mom are nice—I mean, both of you have jobs helping people, and you were always the most popular teacher in the school, and—"

"I think you're a little prejudiced on that one," Dad said. "Not that I don't appreciate the loyalty, but . . ."

"But you *were*!" Marin said.

"I also got to teach the one class where everyone played games all the time," Dad said.

"Yeah, but there are kids who hate sports, and they still loved *you*," Marin said. "Anyway, you have good things happen to you, too. You and Mom love each other, and you don't fight—well, not very often—and Mom got that great new job, and Owen was born, and . . ."

"You do remember that I'm driving home from my best friend's funeral, right?" Dad asked quietly.

"Oh, sorry! Sorry! I mean, I remember, but . . ."

But Marin had gotten so lost in thinking about Ashlyn and Kenner, she had kind of forgotten about Uncle Pete.

Marin waited for Dad to fill in the silence, but for a long moment, he just stared out the window at the dark billboards zipping past.

"Dad?" Marin said.

"I'm just taking a second here, to figure out how to put this," Dad said.

And that was totally not like Dad. He never needed time to think before he talked.

They passed two exits in silence before Dad finally said, "Look, I'm flattered that you think your mother and I have such . . . golden lives . . . and are such nice people. And we do love each other—and you and Owen—and we have been very, very fortunate. But even good changes in someone's life can be a challenge, and maybe we've done a little too well at hiding how much of a stretch it's been for us to deal with a move and a new baby and your mother's new job—and my job search—all at once. Maybe we thought we were a little too much like Superman and Superwoman, and believe me, we *aren't*. It's been hard, honey, and some days, we are just barely holding it together."

Marin thought about Dad yelling, "We're the In Family!" from the top of the mountain on their hike their first weekend in Pennsylvania, and Mom yelling, "We're in love!"

Maybe it really had sounded more like they were trying to convince themselves that everything was going great, rather than that they were bragging.

Marin thought about Mom saying, that first Sunday, "I *need* to go to church."

"What kind of parents were we, if we didn't even notice all last school year that you were having problems with Kenner?" Dad asked.

"That wasn't your fault," Marin muttered.

"Let me tell you a story about your uncle Pete," Dad said. "Do you remember what I wanted to be when I was eighteen?"

"A professional football player," Marin said, as if she was reciting some fact from school she'd memorized back in kindergarten or first grade.

That was because Dad talked about wanting to be a football player the first day of school every single year. He had a whole routine where he'd ask, "Do I look tall enough to be a football player? Do I look *big* enough?" And then he'd say, really fast, "The average weight for someone in the NFL is about two hundred fifty pounds, so *please* do not say yes to that!"

"So you know I failed at that, right?" Dad asked. "And I got cut from being a walk-on for my college football team—they didn't even want me sitting on their bench!"

"Yes, Dad," Marin said. "Every kid at Alcott knows the end of that story—how you are a million, kazillion times happier because you found out what you were really supposed to do, being a teacher and showing kids how to have fun getting exercise and being healthy."

"Maybe I never told you enough about the *middle* of that story," Dad said. "How I was so depressed that I didn't get out of bed for a week. I didn't eat. I barely slept—honestly, I think all I did was cry. I think if there was some way to hold a cry-off—the way I acted then, the way Owen cries when he's having a really bad day or night—I would have won. I probably cried more than the most colicky baby ever!"

"Dad, you're being silly again," Marin said. "Exaggerating, like you do when you ask kids if they think you weigh two hundred and fifty pounds."

Dad thumped his hand against the steering wheel.

"I think I'm not telling this the right way," he said. "You need to take me seriously on this one. I was in a bad way."

The sadness had crept back into his voice. He still sounded like himself, but like a version that had spent the day before at his best friend's funeral.

"I don't know what would have happened if it hadn't been

for Pete," Dad said. "I probably would have dropped out of school. Or flunked out. But Pete kept coming by. And he'd been cut from the football team, too. He was just as sad as me. He'd been just as convinced that football was his life, the only thing he would ever be good at. But he'd already had a lot of hard things happen to him—you know his mom died when he was nine, and he had to go into foster care— and he treated getting cut like just one more thing he had to deal with. Like he was *still* a football player, and it was just a matter of getting back up after he'd been tackled. So he went to class like he was supposed to, and he studied by bringing his notes around and reading them aloud to me. He told me to switch into all the same classes he was taking, and he told me that was so *I* could help *him*. And that's how I became a phys ed major. And then one day, he called and said he had the flu, and I had to go to class to take notes for him, or *he* would flunk out—that Pete! That was the quickest case of the flu anybody ever had, because it ended as soon as *I* was okay!"

Dad was crying again.

Marin thought about Ashlyn lying in her sleeping bag and staring at her phone when Marin came out of the bathroom, after Marin had been crying and crying and crying. She thought about Kenner acting meaner and meaner and meaner to Ashlyn and Marin, even on Marin's last night.

Will I ever have a friend like Pete? she wondered.

She thought about Charley, and how, as far as either of them knew, they were the only ones who could see the Remarkables. She thought about how she'd promised him they could fix everything, even though she wasn't actually sure.

Could I ever be *a friend like Pete?*

THIRTY-ONE

It was already dark when Marin and Dad pulled into the driveway back at their home in Pennsylvania. They'd hit road construction near Cleveland, and lost a lot of time inching forward in bumper-to-bumper traffic, barely covering a mile or two in an entire hour. But Mom had left the porch light on, and Marin was surprised at how her heart leaped when she and Dad turned the corner and she could see the peak of their roof and the flower bushes huddled against their walls and the swoop of the curtains in their front window.

They'd only lived in that house for a little over a week, but it looked so familiar already. It was home.

Because Mom and Owen were there.

"Do you suppose Owen has grown since we left?" Marin asked.

"Let's go *see*," Dad said.

He opened his car door and Marin opened hers, and they took off their seat belts and ran. They didn't even bother shutting the doors behind them; they were too busy racing for Mom and Owen.

And then Mom opened the front door and stood in the doorway holding Owen. He did look older—wiser, too, maybe—and he let out a little "Ooh," at the sight of Dad and Marin, as if he totally remembered them.

"I missed you so much," Mom said, gathering both Dad and Marin into a hug. "I'm so glad you're back."

Marin's face was smashed between Dad's armpit and Owen's chubby leg, and Mom's hand kept thumping and thumping on her back, like a heartbeat. Marin lifted her head a little, and Owen's dark eyes stared right into hers. How was it that babies could look totally innocent and totally as though they knew every secret in the universe, all at once? Owen smiled a smile that belonged only to the two of them. *Look at us,* he seemed to be saying. And Marin wanted to say back, *Oh, yes, I'm looking. You and me, brother and sister, in this bubble of Mom and Dad's hug. And it used to just be me, but, oh, Owen, I'm glad you're here, too; I'm glad we've got each other and Mom and Dad. . . .*

Marin tilted her head back a little more, and she could see that Mom and Dad were cheek to cheek, their faces buried on each other's shoulders. Mom was saying, "I'm so sorry I didn't go with you. The whole time you were away, I thought about you," and Dad was saying, "No, no—everyone understood. It made sense. I just couldn't think before. I was just so . . . so . . ."

"Sad," Mom said. "You had every right to be sad."

Maybe they had had a big fight about Uncle Pete's funeral, but it was over now. Marin could see that, too, just as she could feel the bubble of their love around her and Owen. This hug, and Mom and Dad apologizing to each other . . . that was how the Plucketts were as a family.

Uncle Pete's boys don't have this anymore, Marin thought. *Not with both their parents, ever again. And Kenner probably didn't have this with her parents when they were having problems. And then she was sick and scared and lashing out. . . .*

Marin was afraid thinking about Kenner would bring back all her guilt and shame and anger, but it didn't. She just felt a little pang for Kenner.

But what could she do about Kenner when Kenner was still in Illinois and Marin was in Pennsylvania?

Then Marin thought, *Charley doesn't have this either, with his parents. . . .*

But she and Charley could fix that. Couldn't they?

THIRTY-TWO

Even exhausted from the long drive, Marin still woke up early the next morning. Everyone else was still sleeping, so she slipped downstairs and left a note for Mom and Dad: **Going outside. I'll be back for breakfast!**

Outdoors, the grass was still tipped with dew, and the air was cool for June.

"Life in the mountains," Marin whispered to herself, and shivered. She considered going back for a jacket to pull over her running shorts and T-shirt, but she decided she'd warm up as she walked. She rubbed her bare arms, and took long strides.

Wraiths of fog hung around the trees, and Marin inhaled deeply, savoring the smell of the pines at the edge of the woods. The quiet crunch of Marin's footsteps on the trail echoed a little off the trees. But it was a welcoming sound, as if the woods were drawing her in.

Ashlyn wouldn't like this, Marin thought. *She'd say it*

was creepy. And Kenner would say . . .

What did it even matter what Kenner would say, or what Ashlyn would think? Neither of them was there. Even though Marin had made up with Ashlyn, and sort of understood why Kenner had been so nasty all last year, that didn't mean Marin had to carry them around in her head the rest of her life, ruining things for her.

Marin liked the woods, and that was what mattered.

Charley likes the woods, too, Marin thought. *You can tell. He doesn't* just *hang out here because of the Remarkables.*

As she approached Charley's clubhouse, she started tiptoeing almost reverently, because it felt like that was what the woods deserved. The trees around her had been there for decades, maybe even centuries—the trees had definitely been there when the Remarkables were real teenagers, not just time-traveling visions from the past.

How does it work? Marin wondered. *What makes Charley and me see the Remarkables?*

It made sense that Charley would have a connection to the Remarkables, since Charley's father was one of them. But why Marin?

Marin furrowed her brow and thought hard, but she couldn't even come up with any theories. Maybe that was something else about the mysterious Remarkables that she and Charley would have to figure out together.

She tiptoed right up to the door of Charley's clubhouse and knocked softly. Would he be there so early in the morning?

Maybe his grandma lets him camp out here sometimes, Marin thought. *Or maybe he sneaks out here and doesn't tell her, just as he doesn't tell her about the Remarkables anymore. . . .*

Marin's knocking sounded hollow, and nobody answered. But the door creaked open.

"Hello?" Marin called, tilting her head so she could see through the crack that opened between the door and the doorframe.

The clubhouse was empty. Marin took a step inside, anyway, because something was off.

Each time Marin had seen the inside of the clubhouse before, it had been neat and tidy and homey.

Now there were still little lines of dust by the doorway, as if Charley had gone to the effort of sweeping the wooden floor. But just past the dust, the beanbag chairs were overturned and flung around the room, and scraps of shredded gray paper covered the chairs. It looked like some nesting animals—squirrels? mice?—had tried to make their own home in the clubhouse, and Charley had ripped out their nests.

Marin stepped closer, and saw: the shredded papers weren't any animal's destroyed nest.

They were the torn-up remains of the newspaper Marin had left for Charley.

Oh, and the note I left for Charley, too, Marin thought, recognizing some white bits of paper with traces of blue.

She glanced toward the table in the center of the room. The rock she'd used as a paperweight was still there, still holding down something blue and white. Marin took two steps over to the table, and picked up the rock.

A different note lay beneath the rock now—a note Charley had left for Marin.

Marin could see how angry the scrawled note was even before she could make out the words. The letters tilted and ran together, as if they really wanted to punch one another. Two places had splotches, as if Charley had pressed down so hard with his colored pencil that he'd broken the tip.

Leave me alone, the note said. **Leave the Remarkables alone, too.**

THIRTY-THREE

"No," Marin said aloud.

For a moment, she felt just as helpless and furious as she had at the last sleepover with Ashlyn and Kenner—she wanted to snatch up a colored pencil of her own and scrawl back to Charley, *Fine! I hate you anyway! I'll be happy to avoid you! I would never want to be your friend! You don't DESERVE to have any friends! Or a cell phone!*

But this time the anger was like a tidal wave that washed itself away immediately. What remained was just determination.

"The Remarkables don't just belong to you, Charley," Marin said aloud. "I can see them from my own backyard. Even if I don't know why."

She had to be able to save Missy Caravechio's life. Even if Charley didn't want her to.

Marin put the rock back down on top of the angry note. She backed out of the clubhouse and eased the door shut. And then she took off running—straight toward the Remarkables' house.

Once she neared the edge of the woods and the Remarkables' backyard, she slowed down and went back to tiptoeing. She wasn't quite sure exactly who she was trying to sneak up on—Charley or the Remarkables? But sneaking seemed like a good idea.

The fog had melted away, and the rays of sunlight slanting down through the trees seemed to shimmer more and more, the closer she got to the Remarkables.

Is that a natural phenomenon, or something else that's strange about being near the Remarkables? Marin wondered.

Her heart beat a little faster, as if it were speeding up to match the timing of the pulsing light and the swaying of the branches around her. She fit in these woods; the woods wanted her here.

She had to find a way to make Charley see that. There had to be some way for them to figure everything out together.

She stopped for an instant to gaze up at all the tree branches—what if Charley was hiding somewhere just out of sight?

She could imagine Dad shouting up at the trees, *Hey, Charley! I've got something to say to you! Come down and listen to me!*

But then she thought of Dad's story of hiding in bed when

he was cut from the football team in college.

Maybe Dad wouldn't have shouted when he was Marin's age. Maybe Dad hadn't always been so confident and loud.

Marin kind of wished she could be like Charley, and see what her own father had been like as a kid. Or as a teenager anyway.

Marin *had* seen old pictures of Dad, and Mom, too, and even some old home video of them. Things like Dad at his high school football banquet, Mom being inducted into the National Honor Society. But those videos were so fuzzy, and had such a fake quality to them—*Now, wave for the video camera, Ellen!* Those were fun to watch only because they made Mom and Dad laugh so hard.

Suddenly someone giggled ahead of Marin. First Marin froze, and then she tiptoed as quickly as she could up to the nearest bush.

The Remarkables' backyard was directly on the other side of that bush.

Before, Marin had been cautious about being seen. But today, after Charley's note, she was reckless in her desperation to see the Remarkables. She smashed into the bush, brushing aside branches and ignoring the twigs that stabbed her bare arms.

Now she could see the Remarkables' entire backyard. And . . . she could see the Remarkables. Three of them, anyway. Three girls sat at the patio table, eating what looked like yogurt parfaits and strawberries. One had red hair—it was the girl Marin had started thinking of as Sunny or Sunshine, but now knew had to be Melissa Caravechio.

Missy looked so *alive*. So vibrant, so happy.

Okay, also a little sleepy. She kept rubbing her eyes and blinking dramatically, as if she were trying to get the other girls to notice the effort she had to make to stay awake.

Marin recognized the second girl from the photos she'd found on the patio table the week before: it was the girl who'd been clowning around and laughing so hard with Missy and Charley's dad in the Polaroid Marin had seen right before all of them disappeared. Now the girl sat sideways at the end of the table, and she kept sweeping her thick, dark hair back over her shoulder. And then a lock or two would escape and she'd distractedly shove it back again.

Ashlyn had had a nervous tic for a while where she'd wrap a strand of her hair around and around her finger whenever she was worried. Of course Kenner criticized her for it, and it made Marin's stomach hurt just to think of Ashlyn twirling her hair like that.

This girl's motion somehow seemed like the opposite of Ashlyn's. It was soothing to watch her sweep her hair to the side again and again. It was like part of a dance or a gymnastics routine: graceful. Centering. Marin wanted to just keep watching and watching.

But she made herself turn her attention to the third girl. This girl had her back to Marin, and wasn't recognizable as anyone Marin had seen before. Maybe she'd been in the car that first day, out of sight, and then Marin had been at the wrong angle to see her when she was sitting at the patio table with the whole group.

But, really, all Marin could see of the girl now was her ponytail—medium brown, medium length, and almost as pin-straight as Marin's—and the back of her green T-shirt.

"I cannot believe you two made me get up so early!" the redhead—Missy—said. "It's summertime! I thought we were going to sleep in!"

"We are going to have the best summer ever, and it starts now," Ponytail Girl said, pointing a spoon at Missy. "Why waste time sleeping?"

In reply, Missy picked up a strawberry and threw it across the table at Ponytail Girl. But the girl at the end of the table caught it midair and popped it in her mouth. She grinned triumphantly.

"Amazing reflexes, Priya!" Ponytail Girl said, leaning back and clapping her hands.

Priya, Marin thought with a happy jolt. *Now I know another name.*

Then Ponytail Girl turned to the side to ask the other two,

"Or have you two been practicing?"

Both Missy and Priya started talking at once, their voices high and lilting and happy. There was more giggling. But Marin didn't pay attention to a single word any of them said, because all she could do was stare at Ponytail Girl's face.

Marin knew this face. It was a stranger's face, but at the same time instantly recognizable. Marin knew it as well as she knew her mother's face, her father's face, her brother's face—the face of anyone she was related to. Because this face was definitely the face of someone who was related to Mom, Dad, and Owen.

That, Marin thought, *is what I'm going to look like as a teenager.*

THIRTY-FOUR

Marin tried to make herself doubt.

You don't really *know what you're going to look like in five or six years,* she told herself. *You can't know that for sure.*

Ponytail Girl's cheekbones were a little more prominent than Marin's own, her cheeks slightly less rounded. Her hair was maybe a shade darker, and it had just the slightest hint of waviness, while Marin's was as straight as a ruler.

But aren't those all things that could change as I grow up? Marin wondered. Fifth grade had been the year for the puberty talk at school, and Marin could remember kids giggling when the school nurse talked about how "that baby fat is going to just melt away from your faces." And then the nurse had sighed and warned them, "This will be a *really* long talk if you giggle over every little thing. Even baby fat."

Marin could also remember, in the car on the way home that day, how Dad talked about being surprised that his hair had turned coarser and curlier after he went through puberty. And he'd laughed and said, "I know, I know—it's funny now to think of me even *having* hair!"

Ponytail Girl's eyes were the same deep-set hazel as Marin's; her nose was just as straight as Marin's. Her laughter brought out a tiny little dent—almost a dimple, but not quite—to the left of her mouth, just as Marin's did.

Maybe . . . maybe I'm confused and this is actually Mom? Marin wondered. *Mom from twenty years ago, like one of the Remarkables is Charley's dad from twenty years ago?*

But Mom had grown up in Illinois, and when she interviewed for her new job, she'd made a big deal about how she'd never even *been* to Pennsylvania before.

And, anyway, Marin had seen pictures and video of Mom as a teenager. Mom's hair had always been a sandy-blond color, much lighter than both Marin's and Ponytail Girl's. Teenaged-Mom's face had been narrower than Ponytail Girl's, her nose more turned up, her jawline more heart-shaped.

Ponytail Girl didn't look exactly like Mom. She looked like a mix of Mom and Dad—the perfect blend of the two.

So did Marin.

It is *me,* Marin thought. *There's no question.*

Knowing that, it was impossible to keep crouching in the bushes, watching. Marin had to move; she had to do something. But what? If she ran forward to confront Ponytail Girl and the other two Remarkables, Marin might ruin everything. What if Marin interrupted the very moment when her future self was trying to save Missy Caravechio?

Still, Marin reached farther out, trying to shove aside the last branch of the bush shielding her from sight.

Right before her eyes, all three girls sitting on the patio instantly vanished.

"Okay," Marin whispered. "Okay. I get it."

She spun around and began racing blindly through the woods. She came out in the flattened, treeless section of her own backyard, and immediately scrambled up the little stone wall into the Schmidts' yard beside it. She didn't stop to think. She dashed right up to Mrs. Jean Schmidt's back door and knocked.

"Coming!" she heard Mrs. Jean Schmidt yell from inside.

The Schmidts' windows were open; Marin heard Mrs. Jean Schmidt tell someone, "You keep eating your cereal. I'll be right back." Then Mrs. Jean Schmidt muttered, "Who ever comes to the back door? At eight o'clock in the morning?"

Marin still had time to run away. But she didn't.

Mrs. Jean Schmidt opened the door, a plastic spatula in her hand. The worried expression on her face smoothed out, then bunched up again.

"Why, Marin Pluckett," she said. "Is everything okay? With your family, I mean? Is your baby brother—"

"They're fine," Marin said. She realized she was panting a little. She hadn't combed her hair before heading into the woods; it was probably sticking up wildly, and there might even have been a few twigs still caught in its strands. No wonder Mrs. Jean Schmidt acted like Marin must be having some family emergency. Marin tried to arrange her face to look a little calmer and went on. "And Owen's fine. I just . . . Is Charley home? I need to talk to Charley. It's urgent."

Mrs. Jean Schmidt raised a frizzled gray eyebrow, as if she really wanted to ask, *What is it with the two of you?*

But she turned and called over her shoulder, "Charley? Come out to the mudroom. Someone's here to see you."

"I don't want to." Charley's voice was sulky coming from the next room. "I'm eating breakfast."

Mrs. Jean Schmidt sighed and pursed her lips. She seemed to be making a decision. Then she held up the spatula.

"Marin, would you like to join us for breakfast?" she asked. "I was just about to make eggs."

Under normal circumstances, given such an invitation from someone she barely knew, Marin would have immediately backed away, making excuses: *No, no, I'm sorry. I'll talk to Charley later. When he's ready.* But it was all she could do to hold back from blurting out her secret even to Mrs. Jean Schmidt.

And, based on everything Marin had seen in the clubhouse,

there was no guarantee that Charley would ever be ready to talk to Marin, ever again.

So Marin murmured, "Oh, thank you. I don't really need anything to eat, but . . ."

Mrs. Jean Schmidt held the door open for her.

Marin followed Mrs. Jean Schmidt through the "mud-room," which was really more of a screened-in porch cluttered with sneakers and trikes and bikes and playground balls and baseball bats and gloves. Then they went through another doorway that led into a kitchen. Charley and two younger boys—clearly his twin brothers—were sitting in a row at the kitchen table scooping Froot Loops out of bowls of milk. Splotches of orangish milk dotted the plastic tablecloth.

"Table manners, boys," Mrs. Jean Schmidt said. "We have a guest for breakfast! Say hello to Marin!"

The two younger boys stared at her, their eyes identically wide, and they mumbled equally identical *Hi*s.

Charley scowled and said nothing.

When Mrs. Schmidt turned back toward the stove, Marin tried a pantomime with Charley, pointing to herself and then to him, and mouthing the words *I have to talk to you.* . . .

Charley bent his head lower over his cereal bowl, his shoulder-length hair sliding forward, like a closing door. Now she couldn't even see his face.

Behind Marin, Mrs. Schmidt must have placed butter or

oil into a pan on the stove, because it started sizzling. Using that noise as cover, Marin stepped closer to Charley and said in a low voice she hoped only he could hear, "I saw proof."

Charley froze, a spoonful of milk and Froot Loops stopped halfway to his mouth. Then slowly, deliberately, he turned to face Marin.

"Proof of *what*?" he asked, still snarly, still surly. Still angry. But there was an extra note in his voice.

Hope, Marin thought. *Charley still wants to believe that there's hope, that I really might have good news.*

Marin leaned closer, practically whispering, "Proof that we'll get in with the . . . you-know-whos. Proof that we *can* help."

Charley put down his spoon so fast that the milk splashed and his brothers giggled.

"Grandma," Charley said, too loudly and unnaturally. "I changed my mind. I'm not hungry anymore, so I don't want any eggs. Neither does Marin. We're going outside."

Charley's brothers giggled louder. One began chanting, "Charley's got a girlfriend! Charley's got a girlfriend!" The other began whining, "*We're* not allowed to say we don't want food anymore if Grandma's already started fixing it. *We're* not allowed to waste food!"

Mrs. Jean Schmidt spun around. She pointed her spatula at the two younger boys and said, "Quiet, you two! I haven't even cracked an egg yet, so nothing's going to waste. And boys can have friends who are girls without being boyfriend-girlfriend!"

Mrs. Jean Schmidt's face softened as she turned to Charley. "Sure," she told him. "Go on out if you want."

Maybe it was just Marin's day for noticing resemblances. Because for just that moment, Mrs. Jean Schmidt's face looked exactly like Charley's. It didn't matter that Charley's face was young and smooth and his grandmother's was old and wrinkled. The resemblance went deeper than that.

Like Charley, Mrs. Jean Schmidt still had hope.

And her hope was all about Charley.

THIRTY-FIVE

Charley and Marin made it to the edge of the woods, right by the swing set, before Charley whirled around and demanded, "Okay, now we're far enough away that no one can hear us." He jerked his head dismissively toward the house, as if that was all his grandmother and brothers deserved. "What did you see? What proof do you think you have?"

His gaze was too intense, his dark eyes boring too deeply into hers. But he couldn't make her doubt herself. She lifted her chin high.

"I saw myself," Marin said. "With the Remarkables. Two of them, anyway. Missy Caravechio and a girl named Priya. I saw myself sitting on their patio eating breakfast and talking with them. That means we found a way to get into their time. To a time when Missy was alive. So I wasn't just seeing the past but . . . the future and the past combined, maybe?"

It was hard to know how to refer to the scene she'd witnessed. She didn't even know which verb tenses to use.

"I never told you there was a girl named Priya with the Remarkables," Charley said, frowning.

"Well, maybe you never heard anyone say her name, but there *is*," Marin said. "I saw her in your drawings."

"Okay," Charley said impatiently. "I just . . . never knew that name. Maybe I didn't pay much attention to any of the girls but Missy. Were you telling Missy to check the batteries in her smoke detector every night? Were you warning her about my dad?"

He put a bitter spin on the words *my dad*, as if it hurt to say them.

"No," Marin said slowly. She felt his disappointment like it was something solid between them. She stepped to the other side of one of the swing set supports. "But Missy and Priya and me, the three of us seemed . . . so happy together. Maybe I'd already told Missy everything. Maybe what I saw just wasn't the exact moment that that happened. I mean, of course I'd tell her about the smoke detector batteries. And I wouldn't blame your dad when I did it! He wasn't *trying* to hurt Missy!"

"*How* did you get in to the Remarkables' world?" Charley asked, almost as if he were accusing her of a crime. Maybe of stealing something that rightfully belonged to him. "Anytime I even step foot into their backyard, they always disappear. Sometimes I see *things* they leave behind up close, but never them. Never any of the people!"

Like the Polaroid pictures, Marin thought. *And they vanished as soon as I touched one.*

And yet, in the scene Marin had watched of her older self with Missy and Priya, she'd been sitting in the Remarkables' chair; she'd been holding one of their spoons.

"I don't know how it worked!" Marin shrugged helplessly. "It wasn't like I could ask questions! Maybe, well . . ." She felt reluctant to tell Charley the rest. He didn't even seem happy about her best news. "Maybe it's something that's going to take us a long time to figure out. I think . . . I think the version of myself I saw with the Remarkables was a lot older. Like, fifteen maybe? Sixteen? So maybe it's going to take us five or six years to figure all this out, but I've seen proof now. We're *going* to succeed!"

"*Fifteen?*" Charley repeated, his face going pale. "*Sixteen?* Five or six years? It's going to take that long?"

He glanced back toward the house, then at Marin and the swing set leg blocking him from easy access to the woods. His face reminded Marin of a cornered animal searching for a way out. Then he smashed past Marin, almost knocking her over. He fled into the woods.

"Charley!" Marin wailed, dashing after him.

Maybe Marin knew the woods better than she had the first day she'd seen Charley. Maybe she was just more determined and less spooked. She didn't lose sight of him once. And after about five steps, she knew exactly where he was going: the clubhouse.

He crashed into the door of the clubhouse just a step ahead of Marin, and swung around ready to slam it in her face. She shoved her hand into the doorway, and that stopped him.

"I'm helping you," Marin said. "I told you *good* news."

Charley sagged down against the doorframe, as if his spine had stopped working.

"But . . . five years," he moaned. "Another five years of this? Five more years before my parents are okay? Before they even have a chance to be okay? Five years of me just . . . waiting?"

"We don't *know* that it's going to take five whole years to fix everything," Marin said. She squinted at Charley and tried to explain, even as she figured it out herself. "We just know that I'll be in and able to talk to the Remarkables by the time I'm fifteen or sixteen or so. Maybe we figure it out *today*, and what I saw this morning was just years later— years later for me, I mean, still twenty years or so ago for the Remarkables. It's a little confusing. But maybe after we fix everything for Missy, we stay friends with them, and we travel back and forth to visit them all the time. Or, I don't know, maybe they travel back and forth to see *us*. I'm not really sure which way it works. But wouldn't that be cool? You getting to hang out with your dad when you're *both* teenagers, and before anything goes wrong for him? No, scratch that. Because, if Missy doesn't die, nothing's ever going to go wrong for him. Right?"

She didn't say the words *He won't ever use drugs*; she couldn't bring herself to say, *Your parents wouldn't ever be addicts*. But Charley had to know that was what she meant.

For her, the idea of hanging out with the Remarkables— being *friends* with the Remarkables; being part of their group—was like a dream. She'd seen how they joked around together, how they laughed. They even made it look fun to do homework together! It was everything that she'd longed for without even knowing it, back in Illinois when everything was going so badly with Kenner and Ashlyn.

Marin didn't think being friends with the Remarkables would be like any friendship she'd ever had. It'd be *amazing*. And not just because they were time travelers.

But Charley was shaking his head violently, his hair flying out in a blur.

"You don't know what it's like for me!" he said. "My whole life I've had to worry about my parents. Brady and Brandon are too young, so they don't remember before we came to live with Grandma—they don't remember Mom and Dad at all. They don't remember when they were little and . . . and things were bad. You know that first time you found my clubhouse, when you were holding your baby brother?"

"Um, yeah, but—" Marin was confused by how quickly he'd veered from talking about his brothers to talking about hers. But she did remember how Charley had acted like he wanted to snatch Owen from her, and how he'd crumpled when she didn't let him.

"You want to know why I got so excited when I saw the baby?" Charley asked. It sounded like he was issuing a challenge. "I thought maybe you'd gotten to see a different part of the past than I always did, and somehow you'd seen my family when we were . . . all together. And somehow you'd managed to rescue Brady or Brandon or . . . or me."

His last word was almost a whisper.

"You thought Owen was you or one of your brothers?" Marin asked.

"Crazy, right?" Charley's face was red now. He snorted, as if he wanted to make fun of his own ideas before Marin had a chance to. "Because I should have known, even if it was possible for you to go into the past and rescue us, Brady or Brandon or I never would have looked as . . . healthy . . . as your baby brother. As . . . loved. Because our parents were always forgetting to feed us, they forgot to change our diapers, they didn't give us baths like they were supposed to. . . ."

He choked on whatever he'd planned to say next. Marin's heart ached, and she couldn't have said whether it was for the baby versions of Charley and his brothers, or if it was for Charley right now.

"Oh, Charley, I'm sorry," she said. "I wish I *had* been able to go back and rescue you."

"Well, don't worry, because Grandma did that. Eventually." Marin saw how hard Charley was trying to make it sound like he was over the problems of the past, like none of it mattered anymore. "She saved us. And then she and a bunch of social workers made sure that, you know, Mom and Dad couldn't hurt Brady and Brandon and me ever again. They're not even allowed to see us unless Grandma says it's okay. And it's *not* okay. It hasn't been okay in . . ."

"Five years?" Marin finished for him. She shifted her weight from one foot to the other and searched for the right thing to say next. Tentatively, she began, "It looks like your grandma takes good care of you and your brothers. So—"

"She *does*," Charley said, almost as though he was arguing, rather than agreeing. "I love Grandma. I hate that Mom and Dad hurt her, too. But it's like even she doesn't remember that Brady and Brandon and I had good times with Dad and Mom, along with the bad. There were times when Mom and Dad were all right, like when Dad carried me on his shoulders to see the fireworks on the Fourth of July. Or the times when . . . oh, never mind! You don't care about any of this! You just want to be friends with the Remarkables!"

He said *friends* like it was a curse word. Like it was an

ugly wad of gum you'd want to scrape off your shoe the minute you saw it.

"Charley, I want to be friends with you, too," Marin blurted, surprising herself.

What was she thinking, telling the truth like that when Charley was already so upset?

"I mean, not boyfriend-girlfriend, like your brothers were saying," she added quickly. "Just . . . friends."

Charley did a double take. He took a step back, as if she'd totally stunned him.

"Why?" he asked.

Marin took a deep breath. After everything Charley had told her, she should be able to answer this one question.

"Well, partly, you're the only kid my age I've met so far in Pennsylvania, so it seems like . . . it's logical." Would he think that was pathetic? "And you're the only other person I know who's seen the Remarkables, so we've got something big to share, something *huge*. It just makes sense to work together. To be on the same side. To use both our brains to figure everything out."

Surely, knowing what they knew and seeing what they'd seen, they were supposed to save Missy Caravechio together.

Would he think she was crazy if she started talking about fate and destiny?

But why else had they been the only two they knew of who

had ever seen the Remarkables? Wasn't this meant to be?

How could she *not* think about fate and destiny, when she and Charley had seen time travelers?

"And, Charley, no one else has ever trusted me the way you did," Marin went on, stumblingly. "You told me about your parents. You told me your dad's story. I had a friend back in Illinois, and I just found out, she was going through a rough time all last year, because she was sick and no one could figure out what the problem was. But she never told me. Maybe . . . maybe it was kind of my fault she didn't tell? Maybe I didn't seem like I would ever be a good enough friend to help her, and she thought telling me would only make things worse?"

This was the first time Marin had even thought of that. It was hard to think about how Kenner might have felt. It was hard to know how to think about her at all.

"I think you would be a good friend to tell about being sick," Charley said gruffly. "And . . . I bet my therapist would say your friend was just working through her own issues, so you can't blame yourself. That's the kind of thing my therapist always says to me."

"Well," Marin said. "Okay."

She realized she had sagged against the opposite side of the doorframe from Charley, as if she was having trouble standing up by herself, too. She turned her head to the side, seeing the mess Charley had made tossing beanbag chairs everywhere and ripping up the newspaper and Marin's note.

Charley was staring out at the mess, too.

"What makes you think *I'd* be a good friend?" he asked. He tugged on a strand of his own hair. "Do you know why I grew my hair out this long?"

"Um, no, but—" Marin blushed, remembering how Ashlyn had asked if Charley was cute.

Charley wasn't even looking at her.

"It's kind of hot and itchy, and it annoys me sometimes, but . . . at least it keeps me from looking like my dad." Charley shoved the offending hair over his shoulder. "You know how . . . well, you've seen him as a teenager. If you saw pictures of Dad when he was my age, except for the hair you'd think we were identical twins just as much as Brady and Brandon are. And *I don't want to be like him*. I don't! I don't even want to go to the same schools he went to—that's why I started refusing to go to school, and Grandma made me switch to a different one. I don't want to mess up my life like he did. I don't want to hurt people like he has. Grandma cries about him and Mom when she thinks Brady and Brandon and I can't hear her. And Brady and Brandon *don't* hear. I don't want them to even know. But I hear Grandma crying all the time. Every time Mom and Dad go back to rehab, and there's hope and then . . . there isn't. Every time they're, they're arrested . . ."

Charley was carefully looking away from Marin, his face turned to the side.

"And you know Grandma's the one who told me all about Missy dying," he went on, his words coming out in a rush again. "She said she wanted me to understand how Mom and Dad became what they are. Addicts. But . . . am I a bad son? Sometimes I think, even if Missy had lived, Dad still would have gotten into drugs. He would have found some other excuse for ruining his life! Or maybe he didn't even need a reason. Maybe that's just how he is. So maybe it doesn't even matter if we save Missy Caravechio!"

"It would matter to *her*," Marin said.

Charley waved his hand, as if trying to erase that answer.

"And, see, there it is. Do I only care about my own parents?" he asked. "Am I that selfish?"

"I think you're allowed to care more about your own parents than a girl you've only seen in a, well, a vision," Marin said. "As a time traveler."

Charley's scowl only deepened.

"And then you left that newspaper, and it was like, the same thing that made my dad ruin his life made Missy's other friends do something great," he complained. "It was like that newspaper just confirmed that my dad is a terrible person! He'd be bad no matter what!"

Marin caught her breath. Why hadn't she guessed that

Charley would see the newspaper story that way?

"That wasn't why I left that paper for you!" she said. "I had to go away, and I didn't want you saving Missy before I got back. Not if it meant that other girl—er, woman—Heather Hampton and her friends would be prevented from starting their charity. There has to be a way to keep everything good that happened because of Missy dying, without having her actually die!"

"Oh, yeah?" Charley asked. His expression was flat, his eyes cold. "What if we save Missy, and it *only* leads to bad things? What if we save her life and then she grows up to be an—I don't know—*a murderer*? What if she's *worse* than my parents? I don't think you know what it's like to care about people who do bad things all the time. No matter what."

He brushed past her, headed deeper into the woods. Then he turned around.

"And that's why you shouldn't want to be friends with me." His voice came out as hard as stone. "I'm too much like my dad, whether I want to be or not. Whether we save Missy or not. I always disappoint everyone."

THIRTY-SIX

Marin moved in a daze the rest of the morning. She knew Dad thought it was just because she was tired from the long drive to and from Illinois—and maybe also from staying up late talking to Ashlyn, giggling long into the night. He was extra nice, saying she didn't have to help with any chores or do any more of the unpacking if she didn't want to.

But Marin didn't know what she wanted. She wandered through the house absentmindedly picking up a stray book here, knocking over a stray pillow there. When Owen cried and wouldn't stop—and didn't seem to be hungry or wet or even sleepy, but just in the mood to cry—she told Dad she would take a turn walking him around and around and whispering, "Shh, shh, Owen. Everything's okay."

But then Dad went downstairs to start lunch, and Marin kept pacing the upstairs hallway with Owen, and she stopped saying *Everything's okay*. She started whispering into Owen's ear instead, "You're right. You're so right. There's a lot to cry about. You're so lucky to be a baby, so you can cry anytime you want." It almost started feeling as though Owen was crying on Marin's behalf. "Oh, Owen, you're so smart. Did you figure out how complicated everything is? How hard it is sometimes to help other people, even when you really want to?"

And somehow, even though Owen kept crying, it made *Marin* feel better to hold him in her arms and keep walking back and forth telling him everything. He was so solid, so warm. She told him about Ashlyn and Kenner. She told him about the Remarkables and about how Charley was so mad and hurt about everything connected to his dad. She told him about how Charley was so afraid of being a terrible person that he wouldn't even be Marin's friend.

And then Owen's head sagged onto Marin's shoulder and his eyelids fluttered, and he went from crying at the top of his lungs to being sound asleep. Marin eased him into his crib and went downstairs.

"Owen?" Dad whispered.

"Totally out," Marin answered. "I even managed to put him in his crib without waking him up."

Dad cupped his hand over his ear.

"And we have . . . silence!" Dad declared. He threw his arms around Marin. "Oh, you are the best baby whisperer ever. Honestly, Marin, I don't know what I'd do without you.

Some days I can take the crying and some days I can't. And I start thinking that if only we'd stayed in Illinois, we'd have so many friends around to help us out. . . . Marin, I mean this sincerely—you are better than the whole state of Illinois! No—better than the entire Midwest!"

"Dad, you walked around with Owen for an hour before I took him," Marin said, slightly embarrassed. "We worked together. Like a team."

Dad squeezed her shoulders.

"And, see, you're modest, too," Dad said. "And you know to make sports analogies with me. You're the best daughter ever."

"Dad," Marin said, squirming away. "You'd still love me if I was a bad daughter, right? Even if I did something awful, even if I hurt people or . . ."

Dad jerked his head back and gave her a puzzled look.

"Are you trying to confess something?" he asked.

"No, just thinking," Marin said. "Thinking about other people I know."

"Of course we'd love you no matter what," Dad said quickly. "But . . . we'd try to get you help, too. Is there something you want to tell me?"

Marin considered that. She'd already told him everything she wanted to about Kenner and Ashlyn. And Dad would never believe her about the Remarkables. How could she talk about Charley without saying that he and she both thought they'd seen time travelers from twenty years ago? How could she explain the bond she thought they had, otherwise?

For that matter, how could she talk about Charley without telling things Charley wouldn't want other people to know about his parents?

"No," Marin decided. "There's nothing I want to tell."

She shouldn't have said anything, because Dad kept squinting at her in confusion throughout their lunch of grilled cheese and tomato soup. But he didn't ask anything else.

The day dragged on.

In the late afternoon, Dad looked in the refrigerator and decided they absolutely had to go to the grocery if they wanted anything edible for dinner. Then he peered out the kitchen window, at the low gray clouds hovering just above the tops of the trees.

"I think this is going to be a race, to get to the grocery and back before that storm hits," he said. "Quick! Go get your shoes on! I'll get Owen. On your mark, get set—out the door!"

At the grocery itself, just down the mountainside from their house, Dad made every aisle a game: "Marin, you get the paper towels, I'll get the toilet paper—first one back to the cart wins!"

But when they finally pushed their loaded cart of bagged groceries out of the checkout line, Dad clutching the receipt,

Marin heard a crack of thunder. A split second later, the skies opened, and rain came down in sheets outside the plate glass window at the front of the store. Dad slumped over the cart and Owen's car seat in mock defeat. He pressed his forehead against Owen's and moaned in mock despair, "Two minutes, little guy! That's all the extra time we needed on the clock to win! It was the raisins that did us in—why would anyone hide raisins in the cereal aisle? Why didn't *you* tell us where they were? You knew, didn't you?"

"Dad, really," Marin said. "It can't rain this hard forever."

"Who knows?" Dad said. "Today it might."

Dad inched the cart over toward the door, where a woman with two little boys and a baby was already standing, waiting for the rain to subside.

"Great weather for ducks, huh?" Dad said to the woman.

The woman turned from trying to separate the pair of little boys in her cart. They seemed to be fighting over a box of Rice Krispies treats. The baby she held in her arms looked about the same age as Owen, and the woman had the same desperate gleam in her eyes that Mom and Dad got when they knew Owen was about to start screaming.

There was something else familiar about the woman. Marin tried to see past the jammy handprint on the woman's sleeve and the messiness of the woman's brown hair, which the baby kept grabbing and tugging. Marin imagined the woman in a pretty flowered dress instead of workout clothes.

Then she tried to imagine her twenty years younger.

Because this was Heather Hampton, one of the women Marin had met in the church crying room. One of Missy Caravechio's friends who had started the smoke detector charity.

That meant she was also undoubtedly one of the Remarkables.

Will she *know* me? Marin wondered, a little dizzily. *Will she remember me from seeing me when she was a teenager twenty years ago?*

Mrs. Hampton hadn't seemed to recognize Marin at the church a week ago, but maybe that was before anything about time had changed, before any timeline existed where Marin (and Charley?) had found a way into the past.

Marin hadn't recognized Mrs. Hampton then, either.

How does it even work, the connections between the past and the present and my future self? Marin wondered. *Will Mrs. Hampton remember me differently now?*

Mrs. Hampton smiled vaguely at Dad, but her face lit up when her gaze dropped to Marin's level.

"Oh!" she said. "Hello! It's Marin, right?"

THIRTY-SEVEN

Marin had a million questions she wanted to ask Mrs. Hampton. But Mrs. Hampton was gazing past her to focus on Owen in his car seat.

"And your brother's name is Owen?" Now she looked back at Dad. "Are you Marin and Owen's dad?"

"Aren't I lucky?" Dad said, beaming.

Mrs. Hampton started explaining about meeting Marin and Owen in the crying room at church, and how impressed all the mothers had been with Marin.

Either she's a really good actress, or that's the only *place she remembers me from,* Marin thought.

The baby girl in Mrs. Hampton's arms started fussing, and Mrs. Hampton jostled her up and down.

"You know, when I quit work to stay home with the boys, I thought I was done watching a clock," Mrs. Hampton said. "But this one . . . I get a few minutes behind on her feeding schedule and it's like, boom! From perfectly happy to total wrath-of-God moment in thirty seconds."

"Owen's like that, too," Dad sympathized. "He's so sweet-natured . . . right up until he isn't."

Mrs. Hampton cast an anxious glance toward the rain outside, which, if anything, had started coming down harder.

"I may just have to make a run for it," she said. She glanced back over her shoulder. "I think everyone else in the grocery store will appreciate me for it, so they don't have to hear this little one screaming."

The two little boys in Mrs. Hampton's cart started whining, "We don't want to get wet!" "We hate water!" They puckered up their faces like they were about to cry, too.

"Yeah, I know," Mrs. Hampton muttered.

"Look," Dad said. "I know you just met me, but Marin can vouch for me, and you already know she's a good kid. If you give me your keys and tell me where your car's parked, I'll leave Marin and Owen here—as collateral, you might even say—and I'll run out to your car and then pull your car up to the curb." He pointed out the window. "I'll park it right there, under the overhang, and you can take your kids out to the car and load your groceries without any of you getting wet. And then you'll get your baby home to feed her in peace."

"I can't ask you to do that," Mrs. Hampton said. "You've got your own kids and groceries to worry about."

"They're fine," Dad said. "Marin's like a junior parent, and

Owen already had *his* total meltdown moment for the day. My wife would be mad at me if I *didn't* offer to help another mother. And I promise, I'm not a car thief."

Mrs. Hampton laughed.

"You want to steal a twelve-year-old minivan with dried-up Cheerios in all the drink holders, have at it," she said. The baby in her arms started fussing louder. She reached into her purse and pulled out her keys. "Thank you. I accept."

"As luck would have it, I already own a twelve-year-old minivan, so it's all good," Dad said, taking the keys.

Mrs. Hampton pointed out her minivan in the parking lot, and Dad dashed out into the pouring rain.

And then Marin was alone with Mrs. Hampton. Or, with Mrs. Hampton, two babies, two little boys, and two carts full of groceries.

"My husband and I wanted to have our kids close together so they'd have each other as playmates, but your parents look a lot smarter than us right now," Mrs. Hampton said, continuing to jostle the squirmy, fussy baby in her arms. "Is your mom as nice as you and your dad? I think we need to get to know your whole family. Maybe as Becca and Owen grow up, they'll be friends."

If she remembered me from twenty years ago, wouldn't she say so now that Dad's gone? Marin wondered.

But Heather Hampton wasn't actually one of the

Remarkables Marin had seen alongside her teenaged self. Maybe Marin's future self had met only two of the Remarkables from the past, Missy and Priya.

Could it be because Missy's dead, and we wouldn't meet now, so it doesn't mess up time in any way? Marin wondered. She didn't understand how anything worked with time travel or the Remarkables. But it seemed like it could get really messy, if people's paths crossed at different ages, in different times. *And Priya . . .*

Marin had no idea what had happened—or was going to happen—to Priya. Priya wasn't one of the women who'd been mentioned in the newspaper story about the charity Mrs. Hampton and her friends had started in Missy Caravechio's memory.

But Mrs. Hampton was standing right there beside Marin. Surely *she* would know what happened to Priya.

Marin felt even more tongue-tied than usual.

"I—I saw the article about you in the newspaper," she began haltingly. "That's really nice, what you and your friends do, helping people get smoke detectors."

"Oh, thank you," Mrs. Hampton said, looking embarrassed. Her baby—Becca?—grabbed for her hair again and she had to yank her head sideways to pull away. "I think the reporter made it sound like we've done more than we really have."

"But wasn't it, like, five hundred smoke detectors you gave

away?" Marin asked. "That's a lot."

Mrs. Hampton stared off into the rain.

"Most of that was in the first few years after Missy died," she said. "We're just kind of struggling along now, all of us pulled in so many directions at once." She waved her free hand at the little boys in her cart, who now seemed to be pulling apart pieces of Rice Krispies treats and using them to decorate the back of their baby sister's car seat. "Between you and me, I'm not sure we're going to be able to pull off that fund-raiser in the fall, with just the four of us."

"What about the rest of the, uh . . ." Marin had to stop herself from saying, *the Remarkables*. She settled for: "the other people who were friends with Missy?"

"They're not really available to help," Mrs. Hampton said, frowning as she rocked her baby back and forth more and more frantically. The baby screwed up her face like she really was about to scream. "They've got their own . . . issues."

Was Mrs. Hampton just talking about Charley's dad? Or did she mean Priya and the other Remarkables, too?

Marin saw that out in the parking lot, Dad had reached a light blue minivan and was dashing around to the driver's side of the car. She only had a few more moments with Mrs. Hampton.

But Marin couldn't just blurt out, *What about Priya? Where's she now?* Marin wouldn't be able to explain even knowing the name.

"Maybe . . . maybe you could get other people to help with the fund-raiser just because they think it's a good cause, even if they never knew your friend who died," Marin said a little desperately. An idea occurred to her that could help everyone. "My mom just started working at the college, and maybe one of the student groups would want to help out. I could introduce you to my mom at church sometime." If Mom and Mrs. Hampton became friends, Marin would see her more. Surely that would give Marin a chance to ask about Priya.

She remembered how busy Mom already was with everything at the college.

"Or . . . maybe you could make it a church project," Marin added. "Maybe my family will join your church, and we could help that way. I bet a lot of people at your church would want to help. Like the other woman who was in the crying room last Sunday—Oliver's mom? I bet she'd help!"

Mrs. Hampton stopped jostling her baby for a minute.

"That's . . . that's a really good idea," she mumbled. "I guess we just never thought anyone else would care as much if they didn't know Missy."

Marin saw the light blue van driving toward them, its tires slicing through the flooded parking lot and throwing up flares of water. She really wanted to know about Priya *now*, not sometime possibly in the future if Mom or Dad *maybe* decided to join Mrs. Hampton's church and *maybe* decided to help with her charity.

"The picture of you and your friends in the paper was kind of blurry," Marin said, racking her brain for a way to bring up Priya. "Were those *all* of your best friends in high school? Besides Missy, I mean . . . And are those still your best friends?"

And then Marin's face burned with embarrassment. She didn't even know Mrs. Hampton, and it was almost like Marin was asking, *How many friends do you have?*

But Mrs. Hampton's baby chose that moment to slam one of her madly waving fists right into Mrs. Hampton's jaw. Mrs. Hampton winced and muttered, "Yeah, yeah, future prizefighter here," before shifting the baby's position and glancing dazedly back at Marin to ask, "I'm sorry. What did you say?"

Dad was almost at the curb now. Marin stopped caring if her questions sounded normal.

"What about Priya?" she asked. "Wasn't one of your high school friends named Priya?"

Mrs. Hampton's confused squint deepened.

"No, I've never known anyone named—" Mrs. Hampton began. Just then the slightly larger preschooler in Mrs. Hampton's cart bit a chunk of Rice Krispies treat from the other's thumb, and evidently caught some skin, too. The smaller preschooler began howling. "Michael Ryan Hampton, why did you do that?" Mrs. Hampton scolded. Then her voice softened, "Benji, are you okay? I'm sure Mikey didn't mean to . . ."

The baby in her arms took her brother's squawling as a cue to join in. Then the scolded boy started screaming, too: the smaller boy had bitten him back.

"Benji!" Mrs. Hampton exclaimed. "Oh, Marin, sorry, I've got to get these guys out of here," Mrs. Hampton began shoving her cart one-handedly toward the door. "Hope to see you again at—"

Marin was pretty sure Mrs. Hampton's last word was *church,* just as she was sure the last word she was going to say before her sons bit each other was *Priya.*

She was sure Mrs. Hampton was claiming she'd never known anyone named Priya.

But how could that be? How could Mrs. Hampton not have known Priya in high school?

Wasn't Marin absolutely, one hundred percent certain they'd both been Remarkables?

THIRTY-EIGHT

Marin stood so frozen and confused that she didn't even see when Dad pulled their own minivan up to the curb. He had to get out and walk through the automatic sliding doors back into the grocery and call, "Marin? Marin? Is something wrong?"

Nothing makes any sense, she wanted to complain.

Instead, she shook her head and numbly moved forward, putting bags of groceries into the back of the van while Dad latched Owen's car seat into place.

The instant they pulled out from under the grocery overhang, the rain stopped.

"Figures," Dad muttered, shutting off the windshield wipers. He used a towel to mop water from the top of his bald head and dropped it to the floor of the van. "Oh, well, at least we met a new family. And look at that sun coming out—Marin, watch for a rainbow!"

Marin couldn't watch for anything.

Maybe . . . maybe I misunderstood Priya's name. Or Mrs.

Hampton misunderstood the way I said it, Marin thought.

It had been loud in the grocery store. And Mrs. Hampton had been stressed-out and distracted by her kids.

But if she hadn't quite heard me, or if she thought I said something *like the name of a girl she'd known in high school, wouldn't she have said so?*

Mrs. Hampton's *I've never known anyone named* had sounded dead certain. Even if she hadn't been able to finish her sentence.

Beside Marin, Dad clunked the palm of his hand against his forehead.

"Ergh!" he growled. "I forgot—I really was going to go back to the library today and check out some books to relearn all the social studies info I need. The day just got away from me, and now we've got groceries that will go bad if we don't take them home, and . . ."

"There's always tomorrow," Marin said, trying to sound encouraging. "You've got the whole summer."

Dad gave her a look that made her feel like it might as well be the last week of August.

Would Marin understand anything else about the Remarkables by August? Would Charley even be talking to her again by then?

It was easier to think about Dad's problems than her own. He switched to staring fixedly out the windshield as he drove.

Was he that upset about social studies?

"Dad, why did you get certified to teach social studies if you don't even like it?" Marin asked.

Now Dad shot her a startled glance.

"Not like it?" he repeated. "Is that what you think? No . . . I like social studies."

"But you don't want to teach it," Marin said. "If you like it, why *wouldn't* you want to teach it?"

Dad was quiet for a minute. The only sounds in the car were the tires cutting across the wet street and Owen breathing heavily—maybe even snoring—in his car seat, which probably meant he'd slipped into sleep again.

"Oh, man," Dad said. "I never saw this before, but you are so much like Uncle Pete."

"What?" Marin said. That was not what she would have expected him to say.

"Uncle Pete was always making me realize what a coward I was," Dad said. "And now you are, too."

"A *coward*?" Marin wasn't sure she'd heard him right.

"Yeah. It's not that I don't *like* social studies," Dad said. "It's that I'm . . . I'm scared that if I teach it, I won't do it right. When I'm teaching gym, if I make a mistake telling kids the rules for soccer, it's no big deal. It's not likely that anyone I teach will become a professional soccer player, and if they do, they're going to have way better coaches than me down the road. But what kids learn about social studies, especially history, that sinks in. Wars, slavery, the foundations of democracy, people getting the right to vote—how you teach that really *matters*. It determines what kinds of citizens those kids are as adults. The stories people tell themselves about their pasts—that's important. That affects how they treat each other now, what they want for the future . . . it's *huge*."

Marin thought about Charley, and how stuck he seemed. It was like he couldn't get over his father's past.

That was history, too.

And Ashlyn and Kenner and the problems we had are history now for me. . . .

She went back to peering at Dad.

"But, Dad, you always said that you weren't just teaching gym class, you were teaching kids how to view exercise and their bodies the rest of their lives," Marin said. "And you always, always, always said, 'Be kind is the first rule' . . . isn't that as important as history? Or—more important? You always said phys ed is more about teaching kids how to show good sportsmanship—and to know how to lose gracefully and get back up from a failure and try again—than anything else. And that all *that* applies to everything about life. Wasn't *everything* you were teaching important all along? Won't what you say be important with *any* subject you teach?"

Marin wasn't sure she was making any sense. But it felt

like this was the answer she should have given back in Illinois, when Kenner asked disdainfully, *Is your dad ever anything but loud? Does he ever stop being a gym teacher?* She should have said, No, *my father doesn't ever stop being a gym teacher. Because he always wants to teach kids to be better people. And I am so proud of him for that!*

She expected Dad to laugh and make fun of her, because *she* was almost lecturing *him*.

Instead, he threw his hands up in the air, momentarily steering with his knees.

"Okay, okay, Pete-reincarnated-as-Marin!" Dad exclaimed. "I surrender! I will quit whining about how my life isn't going the way I planned it, and I will get back out of bed and try something new! And . . . I'll accept that God is maybe trying to send me a sign that he needs me in a different place than I thought, and I'll quit fighting that message. . . ."

They pulled into their own driveway, and Dad reached over to ruffle her hair.

"Thanks for helping me so much with Owen today, and for solving my other problems, too," he said. "Did you notice I snuck a box of brownie mix into the cart in the baking aisle? I thought we'd save that for a special occasion, but . . . I think tonight counts! Let's celebrate you schooling your dad! Want to help me bake?"

Marin gazed toward Charley's house.

"Maybe later," she said. "I think I want to play outside right now."

Play wasn't the right word at all. But it wasn't like she could actually explain to Dad, *I have some of my own problems I need to solve now. At least—I'm going to try.*

THIRTY-NINE

Everything in the woods was soaking wet after the hard rain, and Marin's sneakers were caked with mud before she'd gone five steps past the edge of the grass. When she got to Charley's clubhouse, she tried to scrape off as much of the mud as possible with a stick, but she was too impatient to spend much time on it.

"Charley?" she called. "Charley?"

No answer. Was he hiding from her again or just out of earshot?

After their conversation this morning, her best guess was that he was hiding.

"Charley, I'm going into your clubhouse because I want to look at your drawings one more time," she tried again. "It's important. But if you don't want me to, come down, and I'll explain."

Still no answer. Maybe he truly wasn't anywhere around.

Marin pushed open the door of the clubhouse and tiptoed

in. She was relieved to see that at least Charley hadn't locked the drawer of his table again.

But maybe that was a bad sign—a sign that he'd completely given up.

She pulled out the drawer, and there were all the Remarkables again, drawn in painstaking detail.

Er, no, Marin realized, leafing through one drawing after another. *Only two of them are drawn in painstaking detail: Charley's dad and Missy Caravechio. The rest of them are just . . . background.*

Charley *was* an amazing artist. Even with the Remarkables he wasn't as interested in, he'd sketched in enough that Marin could recognize Priya, again and again; she could recognize the laughing boy who'd driven the car the first day. A lot of the other shadowy shapes looked familiar, too. But as Marin tried to search for a Remarkable who could have been Heather Hampton twenty years ago—not to mention the other three women who'd been in the newspaper picture with her—she kept striking out. Was it just because all four women had probably changed a lot in twenty years? There was a girl who kept reappearing in many of the pictures who had the same shade of brown hair as Mrs. Hampton, but that was all.

And women dye their hair different colors all the time, Marin reminded herself. *Even teenagers do that.* Except for the hair, the girl in the drawing looked more like the version

Marin had seen of herself on the Remarkables' patio than she looked like Mrs. Hampton.

Marin felt prickles at the back of her neck, and she began to shuffle faster and faster through the drawings.

What if . . . what if Charley was actually drawing me, *long before I moved to Pennsylvania, long before he met me?* Marin thought, scanning the pictures more frantically. *What if he saw me as I was going to look with the Remarkables long before I knew anything about them?*

How was that possible?

It's not any more impossible than thinking we saw a bunch of kids as they were twenty years ago, she told herself. *It's not any more impossible than thinking I'm going to be able to meet and talk to teenagers from the past someday.*

Now Marin didn't just have prickles at her neck, but chills running up and down her spine. Another wild thought hit her.

What if Charley wasn't completely right about the Remarkables? she thought. *What if that isn't Charley's dad he was seeing again and again and again—but Charley himself as he'll be in five or six years? What if these pictures are proof that Charley and I are going to travel back in time together to meet the Remarkables?*

If that were true, why weren't there any pictures of Charley and his teenaged dad together?

Was there any way Marin could tell which of the pictures

showed Charley with Missy Caravechio and which showed Charley's dad?

She dropped the stack of pictures.

"Charley!" she yelled. "Charley! Really—I just figured something out! I mean, I think I figured something out! I've got to talk to you!"

Marin heard nothing but the wind outside. She shoved the pictures back into the drawer and ran out of the clubhouse.

She had to find Charley.

FORTY

Marin started to head back toward the Schmidts' house, but then she saw footprints in the mud. They weren't her footprints from before—these were a little too big, and they had a pattern of concentric circles embedded on the soles where her own footprints had wavy lines.

And these footprints were headed toward the Remarkables' house.

Charley, Marin thought.

She took off following the trail of footprints, but they disappeared quickly once she came to a part of the woods where the main path held a thick layer of pebbles.

Fine, Charley, she thought. *I know you're going to watch the Remarkables again. I'll find you there.*

But when she reached the edge of the woods by the Remarkables' house, there was no sign of anyone in the Remarkables' backyard or in any of the trees that rimmed the yard.

"Charley?" she called, her voice coming out softer than

she'd intended. The stillness around her was a little too intense. Why weren't there birds or chipmunks or squirrels chirping and squawking? Why wasn't there any sound or movement at all?

It was so quiet she could hear her own breathing.

She held her breath for an instant, but that didn't make it so she could hear Charley. That didn't make it so she could hear anything. She had never in her life experienced such complete and utter silence.

Stop creeping yourself out, she told herself.

She went back to the same tree she'd climbed the first day, the first time she'd seen the Remarkables. She nudged the front of her shoe into the little toehold; she scrambled onto the lowest branch and began to climb on up.

At every level she stopped and gazed all around, hoping to spy Charley crouched in one of the nearby trees.

If she spotted him, he'd have to answer her, wouldn't he? He'd have to say something back if she shouted over to him, *What if you were watching yourself in the past the entire time? Maybe you've seen all sorts of proof of your own ability to travel through time—did you ever think of that?*

Marin was concentrating so hard on looking for Charley that she barely glanced toward the Remarkables' yard and house until she was above the level of the roof. Then, through the leaves, she caught a glimpse of bright yellow in the front driveway. Was it a truck? A giant van? A . . . moving van?

She yanked herself up to the next branch and shoved her way through the leaves—and there was nothing in the driveway, no sign of anything yellow, unless you counted the weak, shimmery rays of sunlight starting to break through the clouds.

And . . . isn't that how the light looked right before I saw Missy and Priya and myself on the patio this morning? Marin wondered.

The slanting light—which was more of a gold, now—seemed to fit with the odd, intense hush in the woods. And somehow the light made her feel like she wasn't just holding on to the tree, but *connected*. She was connected to the tree and the woods and the house down below. She was connected to the light and the silence.

She was connected to Charley and the Remarkables.

Reflexively, she peered straight down toward the Remarkables' backyard. There was still no sign of anyone, anywhere in sight. But Marin noticed a small paper banner in one of the flowerpots. She could have sworn it hadn't been there when she was down on the ground.

But it was the same flowerpot where she'd seen a flag or banner the day she'd first met Charley.

This time I'm not going to let Charley stop me from look-ing at it, Marin told herself.

She began climbing down rather than up, scrambling from one branch to the one below it as quickly as she could. On the lowest branch, she bent her knees and jumped directly to the ground.

Only a single row of bushes lay between her and the flowerpot with the banner. Today she didn't bother darting around to find the easiest way through. She just dived into the first gap she could find between the leafy branches. She didn't care that twigs stabbed her, and the wet leaves soaked her T-shirt. She ended up on her hands and knees still mostly in the bushes, but only inches away from the flowerpot. Her eyes were on the same level as the banner.

It was much bigger than the flag she'd seen the other day. It stuck up over the edge of the giant flowerpot, its first three lines of fancy script easily legible:

Congratulations!
Summitview High School
Class of

Marin's heart thudded so fast one heartbeat slammed into the next. This could be proof. This had to belong to the Remarkables. No one would have put out a cardboard banner immediately after the pouring rain Marin had witnessed only an hour ago.

Crazy thoughts raced through her mind: *No way could a cardboard banner last outside for twenty years. No way could it look that fresh and crisp and new after twenty years even if it was kept inside* . . .

Marin shoved branches of the bush aside and tilted her head so she could see the rest of the banner. She subtracted in her head, fully expecting to see a number on the line after "Class of" that was twenty years in the past. She had a clear view now over the raindrop-speckled rim of the flowerpot. But she blinked and blinked and blinked at the year listed at the bottom of the banner. She couldn't quite believe her own eyes. But the number stayed the same with every blink.

The Summitview high school class being congratulated wasn't from twenty years in the past.

It was from seven years into the future.

FORTY-ONE

That's . . . that's the year I'll graduate from high school,
Marin thought, in shock.

She reached out and grabbed for the banner—she had
to show this to Charley. But the instant her fingers closed
around the glossy cardboard, the banner disappeared. She
held nothing in her hand but air.

Still, Marin knew what she'd seen. Ideas clicked into place
in her brain, completely flipping around everything she'd
believed about the Remarkables before.

"Charley!" she hollered, as loudly as she could. "What
if we never once saw the past? Not you, not me—not ever!
What if we only ever saw the future?"

The woods around her weren't silent anymore, but the
only sounds she could hear now were natural ones: birds,
squirrels, leaves rustling in the wind.

Then she heard a door creak open, a door that sounded
like it was opening after a long time of being left shut. She

could hear the stiffness of the hinges.

She peeked through the branches of the bush before her, straight toward the Remarkables' patio. From her position practically on the ground, Marin couldn't see much besides a pair of tan feet in orange flip-flops. Marin had a pair of flip-flops just like those. They might even be the exact same size.

"Hello?" a girl's voice called uncertainly. "Is someone out there?"

Marin backed out of the bush, deeper into the woods. She was ready to admit she'd been the one shouting, but she didn't want to be seen crawling around on the ground in somebody else's yard.

Then she heard a thud down at the far end of the Remark-ables' yard.

"Sorry—were we too loud?" It was Charley—present-day Charley—answering the girl. Who . . . could be anyone. "My friend Marin and I were just playing hide-and-seek. She can't find me."

Marin could hear the little taunt in Charley's voice.

She could also hear how hard he was trying to make himself and Marin sound like normal kids playing a normal game.

"Oh, that's okay." The girl's voice sounded tentative in a way Marin recognized. It was how she'd become with Kenner and Ashlyn when she'd started feeling like the outsider.

Marin began inching along the outside of the bushes toward

Charley. She kept trying to peek out through the leaves to see the girl on the patio, but there wasn't ever enough of a gap to get more than a quick glimpse at a time.

Maybe the girl had dark, wavy hair, maybe her skin was darker than Marin's ever got, even when she'd been out in the sun a lot. . . .

It was really annoying not to be able to see the girl whole. What if she disappeared in the next instant, like everyone else Marin had ever seen at that house?

But Charley is talking to her, Marin thought breathlessly. *He's in her yard, and he's still a ten-year-old. And he can see and hear her, and she can see and hear him. She's got to be real—real* now, *not seven years in the future or twenty years in the past.*

What had changed, that made it so they were seeing the present at the Remarkables' house, instead of a different time period?

Marin was almost to the first big opening in the bushes. She leaped through the gap, launching herself toward Charley. She grabbed his arm.

"Gotcha!" she yelled.

And only then did she dare to look toward the patio, toward the girl.

Miraculously, the girl was still there. She looked to be about the same age as Marin and Charley. She had dark hair that was about the same length as Charley's, and brown skin, just as Marin had expected.

And she looked slightly familiar.

"Want to play, too?" Marin asked. "I just moved into the neighborhood a week and a half ago—I didn't know another kid our age lived here."

"Well, it was true that nobody lived here—until today," the girl said. Her eyes crinkled merrily, and she tossed her hair back, in a way that made Marin picture her using the same motion with much longer hair. "My family just moved in. And . . . my parents expect me to help unpack boxes. I'm surprised they even let me step outside." She rolled her eyes, and that felt familiar to Marin, too. "Maybe some other time?"

"Sure," Marin said. "I'm Marin, and this is Charley. We both live back there." She pointed over her shoulder.

"Nice to meet you," the girl said politely. She started to step back into the house, then turned around just before she closed the door. "Oh! I've never been the new kid anywhere before, so I almost forgot . . . my name's Priya."

FORTY-TWO

Marin kept her hand wrapped around Charley's arm. She had so much to tell him. He shot her a confused glance and whispered, "*That* was Priya? But—"

"Shh," Marin said. "Let's get out of her yard before I explain."

Charley let her tug him back into the woods, out of sight of anyone in Priya's house who might look out a window.

But as soon as they were behind the first line of trees, he yanked his arm away.

"I just figured it out for myself!" Charley moaned. "You ruined everything!"

"Me? What—?" Marin began.

"You *changed* things!" Charley complained. "You got me thinking I could meet the Remarkables, too, and that's why I called back to her—and it was just some new girl from *now*. Who cares what her name is? Who cares if you're confusing her with someone from the past? Who cares who lives there now? Ohhh . . . What if now all we'll ever see here is the present? Can't you feel it? The air's different now. Nothing's as . . . mysterious. What if you made me lose the Remarkables? What if I never see my dad again? At least I had him from the past, before. What if I've lost him completely, and it's all because of you?"

"Charley, no," Marin said, gasping. Quickly she explained about the cardboard graduation banner she'd seen, and how Heather Hampton and her friends weren't in any of the Remarkables' pictures Charley had drawn, but Future-Marin was. Then she got to her theory that Charley might not have ever seen his father as a teenager—he'd only ever been seeing himself.

"Isn't that kind of cool?" Marin said. "To see how happy you and all your friends—er, *our* friends—are going to be as teenagers?"

Charley jerked even farther away from her.

"Who cares about the future?" he asked. "You don't understand. You've got your mom and dad. Always. I've seen how your dad puts his arm around you when you're walking out to your car together. I've seen how your mom kisses your baby brother's forehead every time she locks him into his car seat. You've already got everything! Why do you get to have the Remarkables be the way you want them, too?"

"Charley, I—" Marin began. She wanted to say she was

sorry, as if she needed to apologize for having a happy family when Charley didn't. As if she needed to apologize for being lucky. Or maybe she wanted to say that just because she had a good family, that didn't mean that everything in her life was always going to be good.

Or maybe she wanted to say that friends were important, too.

But Charley wasn't done talking.

"From the first time I saw the Remarkables, I always thought, at least I got to see my father at his best. At least I knew he could be a good guy," Charley said. "At least I had that. And now, because of you, I don't!"

"But what you believed wasn't true!" Marin protested. "You weren't seeing the past, you weren't seeing your dad . . . Anyhow, didn't you already know from your grandma's stories that your dad could be a good guy? That he *had* been a good guy before the drugs? That he felt a lot guiltier than he should have about Missy Caravechio's death, because it was all a mistake, not because of something that he'd done on purpose . . . Charley, I'm really sorry about your parents. I wish you got to live with them the same way I live with mine, and that they could take care of you like they should. But you *do* have your grandma, and it's pretty clear she loves you and she wants everything to go well for you and your brothers. . . ." She thought about the expression on Mrs. Jean

Schmidt's face every time she talked about Charley, every time she looked at him. In the Schmidts' kitchen, Charley's grandmother's face had held such a mix of concern and hope. And love. "She doesn't care that you're not like your brothers. She just wants things to be good for you—she even let you switch schools because that was what *you* wanted!"

Those were perhaps the most words Marin had ever spoken to anyone in a single breath. But there was still more to say.

"And I think . . . I know I was the one who said we could change the past, and save Missy," Marin went on. "But I think the past is off-limits. You can't change it. All you can do is change how you see it." She had a quick flash of thinking about Ashlyn and Kenner. She didn't view either of them the same way she had three weeks ago. "I don't know how we're seeing the Remarkables at all, but it's kind of a relief that we don't have to worry about changing the past, and maybe making everything worse. Did you see in that newspaper article, that Heather Hampton met her husband because of her charity with the smoke detectors? Which she only started because of Missy Caravechio dying? I met Mrs. Hampton's three little kids today, two boys and a baby girl, and they wouldn't even exist if it hadn't been for Missy dying . . . What if one of those kids grows up to cure cancer? Or . . . to cure drug addiction? What if we prevented all the good that those kids might do, because we changed the past? Anyhow, you said yourself, even if Missy had lived, maybe your dad still would have started using drugs, and just given some other excuse for it. . . . Isn't it better to think about working toward a good future than trying to change the past?"

Marin was breathing hard now, as if she'd been running for miles. She thought about how nice it had seemed at first to have the power to change the past: What if she could go back and save Uncle Pete's life, along with Missy Caravechio's? What if she could go back and unsay the words *I hate you!* to Ashlyn and Kenner? What if she'd never had to see the hurt look on Ashlyn's face—a hurt look Marin had caused? Her heart ached a little, and then it didn't. It was like she'd let go of all the things she couldn't change.

Charley's face twisted, and he clenched his hands into fists. He wasn't letting go of anything.

"How could *I* have a good future?" he asked. "How can I even care about the future—or the present—when my past is so—so . . ."

"Because the present and the future are the only things you can do anything about," Marin said. "You can have a good future because the past is *over*. All you can do is learn from it."

She felt a little like she was just repeating what Dad had said about teaching social studies and history.

But hadn't she also learned from her problems with Ashlyn and Kenner?

"You sound like my therapist," Charley said sulkily. "He's always saying, 'You can't fix your parents' lives. The only life you have any control over is your own.' But . . . I never told him I could see the past. I thought he couldn't understand."

"Charley, I really don't think you ever saw the past," Marin said. "I'm sorry."

But Charley wasn't looking at her anymore. He was looking past her, back toward the Remarkables' yard.

No, Priya's yard, Marin told herself. That's how I have to think of it now. And someday in about five years or so, Priya and some redheaded girl and I are going to be eating breakfast out on that patio, on the first day of summer. . . .

Charley's eyes widened, and he grabbed Marin's arm to spin her around.

"L-l-look," Charley whispered.

Before Marin got her first glimpse past the trees, she noticed that the light around them had changed. The rays of sunlight breaking through the branches overhead were softer and more golden than they had been just a moment before. Even though Marin and Charley were still in the shadows, it felt like the light was reaching out to them— summoning them.

And then Marin could see into Priya's backyard; she could see that a party had started there. And somehow that party was already in full swing, even though nobody had been there an instant before.

Without counting, without tallying up any numbers, Marin just *knew*: all of the Remarkables were there.

FORTY-THREE

"They came back for us!" Charley hissed in Marin's ear. "Maybe now you'll see . . . you'll see . . ."

Marin could tell the exact moment when Charley's eyes caught a glimpse of the sign at the back of Priya's house. His face fell; all the excitement drained away. The sign that he—and Marin—were focused on hung above the door to the patio, and it was a larger, fabric version of the message Marin had seen on the paper banner in the flowerpot: the sign congratulated the class that would graduate from Summitview High School seven years in the future.

The message was repeated in smaller signs and banners and flags all around the backyard and hanging in the surrounding trees, which were also strung with miniature lights. There were pictures hanging all over the place, too: pictures of girls playing softball and boys bowling alongside pictures of each group of athletes hoisting trophies; pictures of clusters of teenagers leaning over microscopes or Bunsen burners or computers; pictures of kids laughing over platefuls of pizza or bowls of hummus. . . . Marin couldn't make out every face in every picture, but she could see enough to make her clutch Charley's arm.

"Charley!" she whispered. "I think this is *our* high school graduation party. Ours and Priya's and . . . and the rest of the Remarkables' . . ."

She waited for Charley to argue, but he didn't. He just kept staring forward, watching himself and Marin and their friends, seven years in the future.

Marin could see her future self laughing and tossing popcorn into Priya's mouth as though it were an athletic competition; the redheaded girl she'd once thought was Melissa Caravechio seemed to be keeping score. Marin strained to hear someone call the girl-who-wasn't-Missy by name—she wanted to think of her as Sunny or Sunshine again, but that felt too fanciful now. This was someone Marin was really going to meet someday. Someone she'd be friends with. Wasn't it?

Redhead, Marin told her self firmly. *She's Redhead until I hear a name that's* sure.

But all three girls she was watching in the Remarkables' yard began giggling so hard that every word they spoke was sputtering and nonsensical. Then Future-Charley started darting his head in front of Priya's, catching the popcorn before she had a chance at it. Future-Marin responded by dumping a whole bowlful of popcorn over Future-Charley's head.

Everyone laughed harder.

The crowd in the backyard shifted as people dodged the four teenagers and their flying popcorn. Marin gasped, because now she saw two other people she recognized: Mom and Dad, looking just about the same as they always did.

It's not like it's possible for Dad to get any balder than he already is, Marin thought.

Maybe Mom's hair was a little shorter than Marin was used to; maybe it was a little more streaked with gray. And maybe Mom and Dad each had a few more wrinkles.

But they were laughing, too, and that made them look completely familiar. And then Dad stopped laughing, because one of the Remarkables whose name Marin didn't know— the boy who'd driven the car the first day—came up to him looking very serious.

"I just wanted to say, Mr. Pluckett," the boy said. "You're the best teacher I ever had. I appreciate everything you taught me."

"That means a lot coming from you, Jamal," Dad said. He shook Jamal's hand. "Having you in class always challenged me to up my game, and I'm going to spend the rest of my life bragging that I was once your teacher. I know you're going to love college."

"Wait—was Dad his best teacher in social studies class

or gym class?" Marin whispered. "Which does he end up teaching? Why won't they say?"

Jamal and Dad broke apart as the crowd shifted again; people were dodging a little boy running through the yard with three other kids behind him in hot pursuit. The boy at the front had sandy-brown hair and dark eyes, and was probably seven or eight. Marin guessed that the pigtailed girl running immediately behind him was about the same age; the two boys behind her were a little bigger and taller and probably older.

The boy in the front grabbed Dad and called out, "Parents are base! Now I'm safe! You can't catch me!"

That's Owen, Marin thought in amazement. *Owen as a seven-year-old . . .*

He was going to look more like Mom than Dad at that age, just because of the hair. But as he grinned at the other little kids, Marin saw that he still looked like her, too. The corners of his mouth curved up in exactly the same way as Marin's; his adult teeth were growing in in the same snaggle-toothed pattern she remembered from her own second-grade pictures.

"That's . . . that's my little brother," Marin stammered to Charley. "That's what he's going to look like in seven years. Are your brothers there, too?"

Charley didn't answer, and Marin realized belatedly that he had stiffened at the words Owen had screamed: *Parents are base! Now I'm safe!*

"I'm sure your brothers and grandma are there somewhere," Marin murmured.

A woman broke through the crowd behind all the running children. She draped her arms over the three kids who had chased Owen.

"Okay, kiddos," she said. "Time to switch to a game that doesn't involve knocking people over. Did you see they have ladder ball set up over there?"

She pointed to the side, where colorful balls hung from tiers of PVC pipe. The kids shrieked and ran toward the game, but Marin kept her eye on the woman, not them. The woman had a very elegant short haircut and perfectly applied makeup, but seeing her face in profile made Marin realize this was someone else she knew: the seven-years-older version of Heather Hampton.

"Don't worry," Mrs. Hampton told Mom and Dad. "I made sure it was the Nerf version before I said anything."

"I didn't doubt your parenting instincts for a minute," Mom said, smiling in a way that made Marin think, *Those two became friends, too. Really, really good friends.*

"Where are the rest of the guests of honor?" Mrs. Hampton asked Jamal.

Jamal pointed toward Future-Marin, Future-Charley, Future-Priya, and Redhead. Mrs. Hampton turned and, to Marin's surprise, threw her arms around all of them, including Jamal.

"You," she said. "I'll start with the five of you . . . I know all the graduation speakers talked about how your class is going to go out and make a difference in the world, but I'm here to tell you, you already have. The way you took over my charity seven years ago when my friends and I couldn't handle it anymore . . . How many smoke detectors have you given away since then?"

Future-Charley was the one who answered.

"Three thousand," he said. "Do you want to hear the Rotary speech I gave about Missy's Memory and all the good it's done?"

"Charley!" Marin whispered, tugging on the real Charley's arm. "Does this mean *we* start helping with Mrs. Hampton's charity? She said seven years ago. . . . Does this mean we start helping with it *now*? Or as middle schoolers?"

"I . . . don't know," Charley whispered back numbly.

Just then there was another disturbance in the crowd: Future-Marin gasped and broke away from Mrs. Hampton, dashing toward another teenaged girl who'd just stepped into the backyard calling, "Where is she? Where's Marin?"

This girl had light brown hair tipped in blue; she wore clothes that shimmered in the twinkling lights and were clearly not from the same type of store as Marin's plain, unadorned green-and-yellow sundress. But Future-Marin launched herself toward the other girl screaming, "Ashlyn! What a surprise! I can't believe you came!"

Ashlyn? Marin thought. *That's Ashlyn in seven years? And . . . we're still friends?*

"Well, you come out to Illinois every single year—I thought the least I could do is come to Pennsylvania once for your graduation party!" And Marin was close enough to Future-Marin and Future-Ashlyn to hear what Future-Ashlyn only whispered, "And you know, you did show me pictures of all the cute guys out here. . . ." She winked at Future-Charley over Future-Marin's shoulder. And . . . Future-Charley winked back.

"Whoa . . . ," Charley whispered beside Marin, which made Marin think he'd seen the winking, too.

The redheaded girl tugged on Future-Ashlyn's arm.

"Hey!" Redhead said. "Hey, Illinois girl! Marin belongs to us now! She's been my friend since the first day of sixth grade. I wouldn't have survived middle school without her!"

"Oh, yeah?" Future-Ashlyn didn't let go of Future-Marin's shoulders. "Marin's been my friend since preschool. I win!"

"Good thing we all learned how to share in kindergarten." Redhead laughed, and Marin realized it was all a joke. Redhead threw her arms around Future-Ashlyn and Future-Marin. "It's so nice to meet someone we've heard so much about!"

As she stared out at the party that wouldn't happen for real for another seven years, Marin's heart felt so full she thought she might cry—with joy, with hope, with awe. Did Charley feel the same way? She turned her head to look at him, and realized his *Whoa* hadn't been about the winking. He was gazing past the hugging girls, toward a cluster of people making slow progress through the crowd.

Marin recognized Charley's grandmother. Mrs. Jean Schmidt was more hunched over, her face a lot more wrinkled. But she moved as briskly as ever, and she absolutely beamed at Future-Charley.

The two tall, gangly teenagers behind her had to be Charley's brothers, Brady and Brandon.

And behind them were a man and a woman who stepped so carefully that it didn't seem like they trusted the ground beneath them. Or maybe they didn't trust their own legs to keep walking forward. They looked a lot older than either of Marin's parents; the lines on their faces were deeply etched. But both the man and the woman were beaming at Future-Charley with the same pride that painted Mrs. Jean Schmidt's face.

Future-Charley rushed over to the couple, and the man reached up and took Future-Charley's face in his hands.

"You've done so well in high school," the man said. "So much better than I did at your age . . ."

"That's all in the past," Future-Charley answered. "You're doing great now."

"Dad!" Charley cried beside Marin. He dashed forward, and the instant his foot touched the grass of the backyard, everyone else vanished.

The yard was empty once more.

Charley collapsed to the ground.

FORTY-FOUR

"Charley!" Marin called.

She scrambled toward Charley, but he was already shoving himself back into the woods, away from the yard. But not away from Marin. He was moving closer and closer to her.

"I'm sorry! I'm sorry!" he moaned, hiding his face against his own shoulder, as if in shame. "I lost it—I was the one who made everyone disappear!"

"That's okay," Marin said, putting her arm around his shoulder and patting Charley's back. It was the same motion she used with Owen when he was on the verge of wailing.

Charley stopped scooting backward. He and Marin ended up crouched against a downed log barely hidden from the edge of Priya's yard.

For it was definitely Priya's yard again—her yard *now*. There was no hint of any other time period, no hint that any party had or ever would happen there. Even the sunlight seemed clear again, perfectly normal for June in a

Pennsylvania woods after a storm.

Charley buried his face in his hands. His shoulders shook. For a long moment, Marin just sat there beside him, patting his back as though he were a tiny, wailing infant.

Finally he looked up. He wiped his eyes on the sleeve of his T-shirt.

"Thank you for not . . . asking questions," he said. "You know those were my parents, right?"

"I thought so," Marin whispered. "I'm sorry. About everything. But really, it was okay for me that it ended. I think I saw everything I needed."

Ashlyn and I totally made up, she thought. *Even living in separate states, we stayed friends. And . . . I'm going to have friends here. And help Mrs. Hampton, too?*

"Maybe I saw everything I needed, too," Charley said, sounding dazed. "My parents are still going to be alive in seven years. That's . . . that's a lot."

Marin reached down and squeezed his hand. Her head spun. Charley hadn't ever said to her before, *I'm afraid my parents will die.* But of course he was. There didn't seem to be enough words in the world for her to tell him how sorry she was about that. About all of it. But maybe the hand squeeze was enough, because Charley squeezed back. Then he pulled his hand away to brush his hair out of his face. He turned and faced her directly.

"Thank you for not saying my parents looked awful," Charley said. "But . . . will they *really* still be alive in seven years? And they'll be healthy enough that Grandma will let them see Brady and Brandon and me again? I wish I knew . . . are they well enough in seven years that Brady and Brandon and I can live with them? Or will we always live with Grandma? How *soon* are they going to get well enough that I can see them again?"

"Maybe you're not supposed to know that yet," Marin said. "Or maybe you'll find out the next time we see the Remarkables. . . ."

"That was a *graduation* party," Charley said. "Do you really think we'll ever see them again? *I* don't." His voice sounded like a door slamming, and his expression was hard as rock. But then it softened. "I mean, not until we *are* them."

"You see what I mean," Marin said. "You see they're our future, not your dad's past. Or . . . Missy Caravechio's."

For a moment, she felt a pang. She no longer believed they could save the girl's life or erase Charley's father's guilt. The tragedy from twenty years ago could never be corrected. But, if she could believe the scene she'd just witnessed, she and Charley and their future friends were going to do something great in memory of Missy Caravechio.

That alone was amazing.

But could she truly believe the scene she'd just watched?

Or the other views she'd had of the Remarkables?

That birthday sign I saw in the Polaroid pictures—it could have really said "Happy birthday, Marin." The scene with Priya and the redheaded girl eating breakfast on the patio . . . It looked like we were such good friends. . . .

"Do you think . . . do you think *everything* we saw was real?" Marin asked Charley. "It always *looked* real. But you watched the Remarkables for a lot longer than I ever did. Did we just want to imagine people being happy—*us* being happy? Is it just what we want to believe is coming for us? Or is it really going to happen for sure?"

"I don't know about the *sure* part," Charley said slowly. "But I think it's possible. I think it *could* happen. *We* can make it happen. The parts about us, anyway. The rest of it . . . what my parents do . . ."

"And what my friend Ashlyn does . . . ," Marin whispered.

"Well, I guess it's possible that all the other people around us will do good things in the future, too," Charley finished.

It sounded like this was a new thought for him. Marin knew he was thinking about his parents, and how long he'd spent believing that all their good moments were in the past.

Both kids were quiet for a minute, then Marin waved her arm toward Priya's yard, the scene of the party they'd just witnessed—which could also be the scene of a party they might live through for real in another seven years.

"Just knowing it's possible helps," Marin said. "And . . . that's enough for me."

Slowly Charley began nodding.

"Me, too," he said, sounding surprised, as if even he hadn't expected that to be his answer. Then he repeated the words, sounding stronger and more certain. "Me, too."

EPILOGUE

It was the first day of sixth grade, and Marin was ready.

She'd gotten up early and pulled on jeans and a soft green shirt that had come in the mail only the week before. The package had been labeled *From your BFF in Illinois!* and *Here's what you need to wear on the first day of school!*

Seeing the package, Marin had muttered, "Ashlyn's not even in the same state as me, and she *still* thinks she gets to tell me what to wear?"

Mom was in the kitchen, too—it had been a Saturday morning—and Marin complained directly to her, "This is going to be something sparkly and glittery and totally what Ashlyn would wear, not me at all."

Somehow over the past several weeks it had become possible to tell Mom, as well as Dad, about how upset Marin had been with Ashlyn and Kenner in fifth grade.

"You don't have to wear anything you don't want to wear," Mom had said patiently as she lifted Owen to her shoulder to pat his back and let him burp. "But you should open it at least. I'm sure Ashlyn thinks she's being kind."

And then Marin had opened the package—and the shirt was plain and simple, without a single ruffle or bow or sparkle. But the fabric was cut at an angle, and somehow that made the shirt seem more grown-up than any of the clothes Marin already owned.

It seemed like a middle school shirt.

"This . . . this is perfect," Marin said. "It's even soft and comfortable, not scratchy. . . ."

Mom gave her a hug.

"Ashlyn *has* known you for a very long time," she said. "She does know what you like."

Now the shirt felt like a hug, a reminder that Marin had lots of people who cared about her. And lots of people she cared about, too.

Ashlyn and Marin had texted a lot over the summer and toward the end of August, and Marin had sent a dozen texts on August 14, the first day of school for Ashlyn back in Illinois. But then the texting had tapered off to once a week or so. Ashlyn had joined the middle school drama club; she'd joined the art club. She had a lot of homework. She was meeting lots of kids who'd gone to other elementary schools.

And that was great.

The evening of August 13, Marin had also typed a different

name into her phone: Kenner's. She'd sat with her phone in her lap for a long time before actually writing the text: **I'm sorry about the mean things I said to you. I don't hate you**. Marin wondered if she should also say, *Sorry about your allergies* or *Sorry about all those medical tests you had to have* or something like that. But Kenner hadn't told her any of that directly, so Marin wasn't going to bring it up. Instead, she finished with: **I hope you have a good first day of school, and a lot of fun in middle school**.

Marin told herself it didn't matter if Kenner ever texted back. It didn't even matter if she texted back something cruel. But a few minutes later Marin's phone dinged with the words **Thank you**. And then a half hour later there was more: **I'm sorry about the mean things I said, too.**

And that was enough. Marin wasn't sure she'd ever see or talk to Kenner again—she didn't have the same history with Kenner that she had with Ashlyn. She had a lot more bad memories of Kenner than good ones.

But she really did hope that everything went better for Kenner in sixth grade than it had in fifth.

Now Marin's phone dinged with the first text of the day just as she was finishing breakfast with Mom and Dad and Owen.

Have the best first day of sixth grade anybody's ever had in the history of humanity! Ashlyn had written.

It was an hour earlier in Illinois than it was in Pennsylvania. Ashlyn had gotten up early just to make sure Marin saw the text before her school started.

I'm telling myself I just have to survive, Marin wrote back. Thanks to your advice, I knew to make sure I could find all the bathrooms when I was there for orientation. So—everything will be great!

Just then there was a knock at the back door.

"Charley's here," Marin said, tucking her phone away and springing up from the table. "Bye!"

"No, no, no," Dad said. "Pictures first, remember?"

This was a first-day-of-school tradition. Kindergarten through fifth grade, it'd been pictures with Ashlyn, and then Ashlyn and Kenner. Today it would be pictures with Charley—and their new friend, Priya.

Marin and Charley had seen a lot of Priya over the rest of the summer. The three of them had explored the woods thoroughly, Charley showing the other two all the hidden nooks and crannies he'd discovered in his years of living nearby. It turned out that Priya loved making movies, and she said the woods were "the perfect backdrop." The three of them worked together to film little skits, even including extra "actors" sometimes: Owen, Charley's brothers, the little kids Mrs. Schmidt babysat, and Priya's older sister, home from her college internship.

By July, Charley had told the two girls that he and his grandmother (and his therapist) had decided he would be fine going to Summitview Middle School with them, rather than staying at his other school. When Charley had admitted, "I am kind of scared," Priya had said, "That's okay. You know what terrifies me? Getting on the bus all by myself that first day!" So Charley and Marin had decided to walk over to Priya's house the first day and all get on the bus together. Maybe it would only be a first-day thing; maybe they'd end up doing it the entire year. Or even all through middle school.

It was a lively progression through the woods to Priya's: Charley and Marin in the lead; Dad and Mom directly behind them, passing Owen back and forth between them; then Mrs. Jean Schmidt hustling Charley's twin brothers along the path and telling them, "No, sorry, this is *not* the time for climbing trees, because we need to be back to the house soon for you to catch the elementary school bus. . . . No, do not pick up that stick and poke your brother! We don't have time for an emergency room visit this morning!"

Charley had skillfully dodged the stick his brother was wielding, anyhow.

"Good reflexes!" Dad congratulated him by high-fiving him so forcefully that Charley's hair swung out in all direction. Absentmindedly, Charley yanked a rubber band from his pocket and corralled his hair into a ponytail.

He'd started wearing it that way a lot toward the end of the summer. Having the hair away from his face made him look even more like the boy Marin and Charley had seen again and again among the Remarkables.

It also made him look more like pictures he'd shown Marin of his father as a kid.

"Maybe my next step is, I'll get it cut really short," Charley had confided to Marin. "Or maybe first I'll let it grow even longer. It doesn't matter, does it? It's not like my hair is really going to make me take drugs or not take drugs. It's not going to make me act like my dad or not act like my dad. It's just hair!"

Marin decided it was probably best not to tell him she would miss his long hair if he got it cut. Even just pulling it back made him look new and different; if he got it cut, she might feel like she had to get to know him all over again.

Maybe that was supposed to happen. Maybe that happened all the time between friends in middle school.

Maybe high school, too.

Maybe even with adults.

Dad started clowning around by holding his hand lower, then higher, staring at it quizzically, and then shaking it out as though Charley's high five had overpowered *him*.

"Whoa, son," Dad told Charley. "I think my aim was a

little off. Did you grow three inches taller overnight? And add several new muscles?"

Marin stiffened at her father's use of the word *son*. She hadn't told Dad anything about Charley's parents, but she was pretty sure Mrs. Jean Schmidt had. What was Dad thinking? Didn't he know Charley had issues with words like *father* and *son*?

But Charley laughed and shrugged, like it was no big deal. Something passed between him and Dad in the quick glance Charley darted over his shoulder.

"Sure, Mr. Marin's Dad," Charley said. "You tell the eighth graders I'm as big and as strong as they are—that'll make it so they don't mess with me!"

Part of Marin's brain thought, *Wait—are eighth graders something else we're supposed to be scared of in middle school?* She was glad she was more interested in wondering about the look that had flowed between Charley and Dad, and the way the word *son* had *not* made Charley bristle.

And "Mr. Marin's Dad"? she thought. *What's that about?*

Dad patted Charley's shoulder, and Charley stood up a little straighter.

Ooooh, Marin thought. *It's like . . . Dad's offering to be Charley's dad, too. Kind of. His neighbor-dad, anyway. Well, that's a good thing. Owen and I can share.*

Mrs. Jean Schmidt caught up with Mom and Dad and held

out her arms to baby Owen, who also reached toward her. He was so much bigger than he'd been back in June. When Marin held him now, he sat up and patted her face.

She watched as Mom let go of Owen, allowing him to snuggle into Mrs. Schmidt's arms for a moment.

"Any word?" Mrs. Schmidt asked Dad. "Do I get to babysit this sweet little boy today or not?"

"No teacher calls in sick on the first day of school!" Dad said.

Despite trying really, really hard, Dad had not been able to get a full-time teaching job in either social studies or phys ed. He was putting a positive spin on the news: he said he could take a year of subbing to get to know the local schools, and figure out where he really wanted to work.

"And, of course, I'll wow them so much as a sub that all the schools will be fighting over me next summer!" he'd told Marin when the last rejection came.

He said it would be much easier not to have to come up with lesson plans or grade papers while also dealing with Owen's crazy schedule and just adjusting to living in a new place in general.

And when he'd worried about having to pay for childcare that Owen didn't need every day, Mrs. Schmidt had stepped up and offered to babysit only when she was needed.

"And if we have to live on just macaroni and cheese and

spaghetti for a while, well, who doesn't like macaroni and cheese and spaghetti?" Dad had asked.

Marin kind of wanted to tell him that sometime within the next seven years he would be teaching full-time again, and become the favorite teacher of a kid she hadn't even met yet named Jamal.

But it already seemed like Dad felt confident that he'd be back to teaching full-time soon. And she believed him when he said he was glad he'd have extra time with Owen and Marin this year.

Just then his phone buzzed. Dad looked at its screen.

"So I'm wrong . . . I guess it is possible for teachers to get sick on the first day! Strep throat—ugh! But thanks to Ms. Suzanne Croce's illness, you are looking at Summitview High School's consumer and family sciences teacher for the day! Wait, what is consumer and family sciences? Is that what we used to call home ec?" Dad raised his arms like he was a bodybuilder showing off his muscles. "They really think they're going to test me as a sub by having me teach home ec? Little do they know I've been the chief family cook all summer! I'm all over this one!"

Marin inched forward, pulling Charley along with her.

"Don't mind him—sometimes he starts believing all the people who say it's amazing that he's been a stay-at-home dad with Owen and me all summer," Marin whispered. "And it is so totally not a big deal."

"Nope," Charley said.

Marin realized he was staring toward Priya's yard ahead of them. They were almost to the last row of trees and bushes. The woods had seemed so huge at the beginning of the summer, but now it seemed like no distance at all from Marin's house to Priya's. It was such a familiar walk.

Marin held her breath for an instant until she saw: Priya's backyard was empty.

"Every single time," Marin whispered. "Every single time I have a moment of thinking I'm going to see the Remarkables again . . ."

Neither she nor Charley had seen them even once since witnessing the graduation party. She was starting to think that Charley was right, and they wouldn't see the Remarkables again until they *were* the Remarkables.

"I don't think we need them anymore," Charley said matter-of-factly. "You-know-who probably knows that."

Ever since they'd seen the graduation party, Charley and Marin had had debates about what had caused them to see the Remarkables from the very beginning. *Was* it time travel, and would they discover some sort of superpower within themselves within the next seven years that would allow them to do that?

Or was it a message from God—a vision, like the kind

Marin heard about at church? (To test out this idea, Charley had agreed to go to Vacation Bible School with Marin at her new church. They'd had fun, but he'd been disappointed that the theme had been "Helping Our Neighbors," not "Weird Visions Certain Prophets Had in the Bible and You Might Have, Too.")

Charley's favorite theory was that "you-know-who" had caused everything: Melissa Caravechio. He'd decided that her psychic energy lingered in the place where she'd died—"like a ghost, but not scary" was how he put it. He said that just as she'd been a good person when she was alive, she must have left behind good energy when she died, and her way of haunting people was to show them good things they needed to see.

"I still want to believe it's time travel," Marin said now. "Because then it's not completely over. Maybe in seven years we'll be able to watch ourselves at our *college* graduation parties. . . ."

"Let's just get through the first day of sixth grade, okay?" Charley said nervously.

They reached Priya's house, and her parents had to exclaim about how beautiful and handsome and grown-up Marin and Charley looked, and how glad they were that Priya already had such good friends, to come over and catch the bus with her.

The adults seemed to want endless pictures, with every

combination of people: just the kids alone, each kid with siblings, each family group. . . . The photo session in Priya's front yard ended only because the school bus pulled up the hill. Dad had just said, "Now show me your goofiest expressions!" and Charley gave Priya bunny ears and Priya pretended her fingers were vampire fangs, just as Marin glanced to the side to watch the bus approach.

Dad's phone camera snapped, and Marin caught a glimpse of Charley and Priya out of the corner of her eye. Their expressions looked so familiar.

It's like in the pictures I saw of the Remarkables. . . . They're growing up and turning into those people. . . .

That is, if you could call making bunny ears and fake fangs "growing up."

"So we want to hug you goodbye, but that's probably not what you want in front of that whole busload of middle school kids, right?" Dad asked.

"Exactly," Marin said. But then she said, "Blow a kiss," to Owen—who was now cuddled in Priya's mother's arms—and he made a sputtering, spitty sound with his lips—a trick he'd learned only the week before.

The bus pulled up in front of Priya's driveway, turning completely around in the cul-de-sac before opening its door. Charley, Marin, and Priya all climbed on. Marin was right behind Priya, and Marin could tell that the other girl's knees were shaking.

"You're not alone," Marin whispered behind her.

"Oh no," Charley said, pointing out the nearest window.

Outside, all the grown-ups—even Mrs. Jean Schmidt, even Priya's parents—were pretending to blow kisses.

"They are so embarrassing!" Priya protested, dropping into the first empty seat she came to.

"Don't worry—nobody else is paying attention," Marin said, sitting down beside her while Charley took an empty seat behind them. "And anyway, everyone else will just think they're waving. Normally, I mean."

"No, I can tell they're trying to embarrass you," a boy across the aisle said, glancing up from a book he'd been reading. "But don't feel bad—my parents had this whole goofy dance *they* did at the bus stop. . . . Oh, never mind."

He went back to his book.

Marin stared at the boy. He had braces and slicked-back hair, and even though it was a warm day, he was wearing an actual suit jacket with leather patches on the elbows. He looked like a middle school boy disguised as a college professor. And there was something familiar about his face.

Marin turned around to Charley and mouthed a name: *Jamal?* She tilted her head toward the boy with the book.

Charley's eyes widened. Then, quickly, before the bus started moving again, he crossed the aisle toward Jamal.

"Mind if I sit with you?" Charley asked.

"No problem," Jamal said.

He didn't go back to reading his book this time. He started telling Charley how his parents' weird dance resembled string theory in physics, and . . .

This is how it starts, Marin thought, a chill traveling her spine. *We met Priya, and now we've met Jamal. . . .*

But there was only one Remarkable who'd announced exactly when she and Marin would meet: the redheaded girl who said she and Marin had become friends on the first day of sixth grade.

If Marin didn't meet the red-haired girl today, that would mean that other things about the Remarkables might not come true, either.

For most of the way to school, Marin and Priya rode in comfortable silence—it was so different from how Ashlyn would have chattered constantly. Marin could both miss Ashlyn and appreciate Priya for not expecting any *Uh-huh*s and *You're right*s in the midst of an overwhelming flow of words.

No redheaded girl showed up at any of the bus stops.

Then they were at the school, and an entire sea of kids stood on the sidewalk outside the front door. Marin hadn't realized there were so many kids in all of Summitview.

She couldn't see a single redhead anywhere in the crowd.

A bell rang, and the sea turned into a river flowing through the doors. Numbly, Marin got off the bus alongside Priya, Charley, and Jamal.

"Strategy: Stay Together," Priya muttered under her breath, and Marin nodded.

When they reached the front door, a cluster of adults—teachers, probably—told everyone, "Sixth graders to the auditorium. Seventh and eighth graders, straight to homeroom."

Another cluster of adults stood immediately inside the doors announcing the same thing.

Marin turned to Priya to say, "I bet they're getting really sick of saying that over and over again."

But turning sideways kept Marin from seeing what lay right in front of her, and she bumped into a girl walking diagonally through the crowd headed for the auditorium.

"Oh, sorry," Marin said. But the other girl was turning to apologize at the same time, and Marin got a mouthful of hair.

Red hair.

Marin sprang back and grabbed for Charley's arm.

"My fault," the girl said.

Marin had had trouble seeing the resemblances between the Remarkable versions of Priya, Jamal, Charley—and even herself—and the way they looked right now. But this girl was unmistakably the same redheaded Remarkable girl

Marin and Charley had thought was Melissa Caravechio. Her hair was the same length, and just as curly and bright; her freckles were just as vivid. The only difference was that she looked ever so slightly shorter and younger, and her eyes seemed bigger in her face, with uncertainty mixed into her gaze along with a hint of her usual glee.

"L-l-look," Charley said from behind Marin.

He was pointing not at the redheaded girl, but at the schedule she clutched in her hand.

Marin realized that Charley wasn't upset because he'd seen that this girl was going to be in their math class. He was pointing at the girl's name.

"You're Melissa Caravechio?" Marin blurted out. "For real? But that's—"

Impossible, she wanted to say. *Unbelievable. Crazy.*

"Oh, boy," the girl said, with a little roll of her eyes. "Dad said this might happen when we moved back here, but he only warned me that grown-ups might do this. . . . I really didn't believe Summitview was such a small town that people would still be talking about something that happened twenty years ago."

Marin couldn't speak.

"I'd say I'm the one and only Melissa Caravechio, but from how you're acting, I guess you know why I'm the one and only *now,*" the girl said. "I was named for my aunt, who died before I was born. But I go by Lissy. So, see? I am unique!"

Marin looked back at Charley, who stood frozen in place. He didn't seem capable of speech, either. Then he suddenly blurted out, "I'm Carl Schmidt's son."

Marin wanted to throw herself in between Charley and Lissy. She wanted to protect both of them—and maybe Priya and Jamal, too, who were standing behind Charley looking puzzled.

But Lissy's face lit up.

"Really?" she said, as if she'd just learned Charley was some famous celebrity she'd always wanted to meet. Not the son of the guy responsible for her aunt's death. "I've heard so many stories about Aunt Missy and her friend Carl, and how they were such good friends."

"But my dad was the one who—" Charley said, plowing forward with the grim words as though he had no choice.

"The one my aunt Missy loved," Lissy interrupted gently. "The one no one in my family blames for anything at all."

For just that moment, Lissy didn't sound like a sixth-grade girl. She sounded like an angel or a time traveler, or the forgiving ghost of the aunt she'd been named for. Or maybe she sounded like one of the prophets Charley had wanted to learn about.

And for just a moment, Marin wondered if the fluorescent overhead lights of the school had changed, and become more like the light in the Pennsylvania woods in June.

Then a teacher came up behind them.

"Kids, save the socializing for *after* school," he said, as wearily as if it were the last day of school instead of the first. "Or at least wait until lunch. Into the auditorium, please. You're blocking the hall."

Lissy, Marin, Charley, Priya, and Jamal waited until they were inside the auditorium before every single one of them burst into giggles.

"Save the socializing for *after* school," Jamal repeated, imitating the teacher's voice exactly. And Marin could see how this would become something they said to each other for the rest of the school year (but only when teachers weren't listening). She could see that it might even be a phrase they were still repeating the night of their high school graduation.

"Our first inside joke," Marin whispered to Charley. "The *Remarkables'* first inside joke."

"If we're going to be superheroes," Charley whispered back, "this is part of our origin story."

Marin didn't know if they were ever going to be superheroes. She didn't know if they were ever going to be time travelers. She didn't even know if any of them would ever be any more remarkable than any other teenager. But right now, laughing at the back of the middle school auditorium on the first day of sixth grade—even as she scanned the crowd for others she might soon recognize—she knew these kids were going to be her friends for a very long time. And all of them were going to be Remarkable together.

That made everything else feel possible, too.

ACKNOWLEDGMENTS

Like Marin, I once made a move from Illinois to Pennsylvania at a time when many other things in my life were changing, too. In my case, I was an adult with a husband and a two-year-old daughter. I was also about to give birth to our second child—it wasn't exactly the best time to move to a place nine hours away from our families, where we didn't know a single soul. I had never even visited northeastern Pennsylvania until we moved there. This all happened more than twenty years ago, but I am still deeply, deeply grateful to the people who went out of their way to offer us friendship and help from the very beginning. Thanks especially to Carol, Rick, and Tony Monaco; and Karen Arcangelo, Joy Westdorp, and Lisa Sauder. There's a direct line from their kindnesses of twenty years ago to this book existing today.

Fast-forwarding to the present (more time travel!), I am also grateful to my friend Dr. Tim Richards, who's the medical director of an addiction treatment clinic, and Ronald T. McClain, who's worked in the field of chemical dependency for thirty-three years, who both gave me information that helped in my efforts to depict Charley's attitudes toward his parents in an accurate way.

I'd also like to thank my sister and nieces—Janet, Jenna, and Meg Terrell—who served as extra consultants about what life is like with and for eleven-year-old girls. I don't just appreciate your help—I also appreciate how much we laughed at ourselves, discussing topics like what Ashlyn's room should smell like.

I started writing this book at a time when I was also recovering from a broken wrist, so I have to thank all the people who made it physically possible for me just to type, especially Dr. Paul A. Cook, the surgeon who put my shattered wrist back together, and Angela Rutty, the physical therapist I worked with the most.

Between the broken wrist and some other factors, writing this book meant following an unusual process for me, and I am grateful to both my agent, Tracey Adams, and my editor, Katherine Tegen, for welcoming it into the world regardless. Thanks as well to everyone else at HarperCollins who worked on this book, especially Mabel Hsu, Sara Schonfeld, Kathryn N. Silsand, Mark Rifkin, Allison C. Brown, David E. Curtis, Erin Fitzsimmons, Ann Dye, Emma Meyer, Jacqueline Hornberger, and Aubrey Churchward. Also, thank you to Daniel Burgess for capturing the mood of the story with his beautiful cover art.

And, as always, I am grateful to my family, especially my husband, Doug, and to my friends, especially those in my Ohio writer groups who understand all the agonies and joys of what we do: Jody Casella, Julia DeVillers, Linda Gerber, Lisa Klein, Erin McCahan, Jenny Patton, Edith Pattou, Nancy Roe Pimm, Amjed Qamar, Natalie D. Richards, and Linda Stanek.

You're all remarkable.

TURN THE PAGE TO ENTER

THE TWISTY, MYSTERIOUS WORLD OF

Greystone Secrets: The Strangers

ONE

FINN

The three Greystone kids always raced each other home when they got off the school bus, and Finn always won.

It wasn't because he was the fastest.

Even he knew that his older brother and sister, Chess and Emma, let him win so he could make a grand entrance.

Today he burst into the house calling out, "Mom! We're home! It's time to come and adore us!"

"Adore" had been on his second-grade spelling list two weeks ago, and it had been a great discovery for him. So *that* was what it was called, the way he had felt his entire life.

Emma, who was in fourth grade, dropped her backpack

on the rug beside him and kicked off her red sneakers. They flipped up and landed on top of the backpack—someday, Finn vowed, he would get Emma to teach him that trick.

"Twenty-three," Emma said. There was no telling what she might have been counting. Finn hoped it was a prediction of how many chocolate chips would be in every cookie Mom was probably baking for them right now, for their after-school snack.

Finn sniffed. The house did not smell like cookies.

Oh well. Mom worked from home, designing websites, and sometimes she lost track of time. If today was more of a Goldfish-crackers-and-apple-slices kind of day, that was okay with Finn. He liked those, too.

"Mom!" he called again. "Your afternoon-break entertainment has arrived!"

"She's in the kitchen," Chess said, hanging his own backpack on the hook where it belonged. "Can't you hear?"

"That would mean Finn had to listen for once, instead of talking," Emma said, rubbing Finn's head fondly and making his messy brown hair even messier. Finn knew she didn't mean it as an insult. He was pretty sure Emma liked talking as much as he did.

Chess was the one everyone called "the quiet Greystone." He was in sixth grade and had grown four inches in the past year. Now Finn had to tilt his head way back just to see his brother's face. He also cupped his hand over his ear and pretended to be listening really, really hard. There was a low mumble coming from the kitchen—maybe a man's voice?

"Is Mom watching TV?" Chess asked. "She never does that during the day."

The kids all knew their mother's routine. She never listened to anything but classical music while she worked, because she said songs with words were too distracting. And when she really didn't want to be disturbed, she worked in a windowless room in the basement. The computer down there didn't even connect to the internet.

The three Greystone kids called that "the Boring Room."

Now Finn laughed at his older brother.

"Are you going to stand around asking stupid questions when you could get your answer just by walking into the kitchen?" Finn asked. "Let's go eat!"

He dashed toward the kitchen, dodging both Emma's backpack and the family's cat, Rocket, lying in the middle of the floor. He yelled, "Mom, can I cut up apples? It's my turn, isn't it?"

Mom was standing at the kitchen counter with her back to Finn, but she didn't turn around. She had both hands clenched onto the edge of the counter, as if she needed to hold on. Her cell phone lay facedown on the floor by her feet. Her laptop sat on the counter in front of her, but it was tilted up, so Finn couldn't see what was on the screen.

"Mom?" Finn tried again.

She still didn't turn around. It was like she didn't even hear him, like she was in a soundproof bubble.

This was not like Mom. She had never acted like this before.

Then she began to moan: "No, no, no, no, no. . . ."

TWO

EMMA

Emma had had a substitute teacher that day. The sub had dressed all in gray and had gray hair and a gray face and even a gray voice—somehow, Emma decided, that was possible. And the sub made the entire day so dreary and dull that Emma had started looking for and counting weird things about the day just to keep herself awake.

The thing was, if you started looking for weirdness, suddenly everything seemed that way. Wasn't it weird that the pattern of coats hanging up on the classroom hooks went blue-green-red, blue-green-red twice in a row? Wasn't it weird that the sub could have a gray voice? (Or was that just normal for her?)

By the time Emma got off the school bus and began racing toward the house, she'd counted twenty-one things she considered indisputably weird. To her way of thinking, that actually made the day pretty interesting, and she was excited to tell Mom about the new trick she'd discovered for surviving school.

Then she noticed that the porch light was still on, even though Mom usually turned it off when Emma and her brothers left for school.

And then, stepping into the house, Emma noticed that the living room curtains were still drawn tight across the windows, and so were the blinds on the bay window at the back of the house. This turned the living room's cheery yellow walls dim and shadowy; it made the whole house feel like a cave or a hideout.

Twenty-three weird things in one day. What if that was a normal amount, and Emma had just never noticed before?

She'd have to count again some other day—or, really, lots of other days—to know for sure.

Finn and Chess started yammering on about Mom and the kitchen and TV. Emma joined in and then rubbed Finn's head, because it felt good to do something normal again. Mussing Finn's hair was like petting a dog—you had to do it. Finn had thick, unruly hair with odd cowlicks that sprang up no matter how much Mom smoothed them down. Finn being Finn, he claimed this meant his hair had superpowers.

And . . . now Finn was racing off to the kitchen, shouting about apples.

Emma looked up at Chess, and they both shrugged and grinned and followed Finn.

But when they got to the kitchen, Mom wasn't hugging Finn and reaching out to hug Emma and Chess, too. Finn stood in the middle of the kitchen, staring at Mom. Mom stood at the counter with her back to the kids, all her attention focused on her laptop.

And the voice coming out of the laptop was saying, "The kidnapped children are in second and fourth and sixth grade."

THREE

CHESS

"Mom?" Chess said quietly.

His mother's shoulders shook. And then, as if she was fighting for control, her whole body went still.

Just like before, Chess thought.

Of the three Greystone kids, only Chess remembered the awful day their father died. Chess had been four; Emma, two; and Finn, only a baby. But even Chess's memories of that day were more like puzzle pieces he kept in a box in his mind, rather than one continuous video: Chess remembered the two sad-faced police officers at the door; he remembered the red Matchbox car he'd been holding in his hand when the door opened; he remembered the way Mom's shoulders shook before her back went ramrod straight, and she turned around to face Chess and Emma and Finn.

Now Mom was reaching for the top part of her laptop, as if she planned to shut it and hide whatever it said. Something made Chess stride quickly across the kitchen and grab her hand to stop her.

"Someone was kidnapped," he said. He caught a glimpse of a few words at the bottom of the computer screen. "Three kids in Arizona. Was it anyone you know?"

"No . . . ," Mom whispered.

Her dark eyes were wide and dazed. The color had drained from her face.

Shock, Chess thought. The school nurse had come in and taught a first-aid unit to the sixth graders earlier that year, and Chess was proud of himself for remembering the symptoms.

It was just a shame he couldn't remember any treatment.

Maybe he was feeling a little shocked himself. It was scary that anyone would kidnap anyone. But Arizona was a thousand miles away. And it wasn't like there would be some crime ring going around kidnapping kids from any family who had a second grader, a fourth grader, and a sixth grader.

"Mom, maybe you should sit down," Emma said.

Hmm. Maybe that was one of the treatments for shock.

Chess shot his sister a grateful look and took his mother's arm, ready to help ease her toward the kitchen table.

"Rocky, Emma, and Finn Gustano were last seen leaving their school, Los Perales Elementary, in Mesa," the voice coming out of the laptop speakers said.

Finn started cracking up.

"Isn't that funny?" he cried. "Two of those kids have the same first names as me and Emma! That's the third Finn I've ever known. Well, not that I actually know this one, but . . ." He slugged Chess in the arm. "Don't you feel bad that *you* don't have the same name as some kid who's famous now? And I bet when they find these kids, they'll get all the ice cream they want, and all the toys they want, and their parents probably won't make them do homework ever again!"

But what if nobody ever *finds these kids?* Chess thought.

He wasn't about to say that to Finn.

"Yeah, I've never met another kid named Rochester." Chess forced himself to fake a smile at Finn. "Or with the nickname 'Chess.' Oh well."

"Maybe you should *sue* Mom for giving you such a different name," Finn suggested.

"Or maybe I should sue for getting such a boring, ordinary name," Emma countered. "Did you know there are three other Emmas in fourth grade? And eight others in the rest of the school!"

But Chess tuned out his brother and sister. Because Mom lifted one hand and pointed toward the laptop screen. The way she held her hand was like a nightmare, like a Halloween ghost, like someone under a witch's spell in a fairy tale. It was like she could only point, not speak.

"We're repeating the information we have about the Gustano children," the voice coming from the laptop said. A photo of a friendly-looking, dark-haired boy appeared on the screen. "The oldest of the three kidnapped siblings, Rochester Charles Gustano, who goes by Rocky, just turned twelve last Tuesday. . . ."

Chess's hearing blanked out temporarily. His middle name was Charles, too. And his twelfth birthday had been last Tuesday.

How could there be another Rochester Charles, born the exact same day as him?

And how could that other kid have been kidnapped?

FOUR

FINN

Everybody was acting too serious. They'd all stopped talking. Even Emma. She'd taken the last two steps to join Mom and Chess at the counter, to stare silently at the laptop screen.

"Hello?" Finn said. "It's snack time—remember?"

Nobody answered.

"Remember how you're always telling me I have to quit right away when I'm playing computer games and you think it's time for me to do something else?" Finn tried again.

He walked over and reached his hand for the power button on the laptop. He wasn't *really* planning to switch it off—he'd heard too many lectures from Mom about not messing with her work. He just wanted to tease Mom a little, until she acted normal again.

Emma surprised him by grabbing his hand. At first it seemed like she was just trying to stop him from doing something dumb. Then it started feeling like she *needed* to hold his hand.

Finn stood on tiptoes and peered at the screen. He saw three pictures in a row, each with names and ages beneath. The kids in the pictures all had brown hair, just like Finn and Chess and Emma did, and they stared out at Finn with stiff school-picture-day smiles on their faces, as if they'd gotten the same warning Finn always got: "Remember, this is your official photo for the entire year, so no goofing off!" The youngest boy, the one Finn was already thinking of as Other-Finn, was perfectly snaggletoothed, with one adult front tooth partly grown in and one front tooth missing entirely.

Finn felt a little jealous. He'd lost both his front teeth two weeks after picture day last fall, and for some reason Mom wouldn't agree to let him have his picture retaken just because of that.

"But Mom, this is what I look like in second grade," he'd argued, sticking his tongue into the hole where his teeth used to be just for the sheer joy of it. "Don't you want to remember me this way forever?"

"Don't worry," Mom had said, laughing and pretending to try to catch his tongue before he yanked it back. "I'm not going to forget, regardless."

Finn dropped his gaze to see if Other-Finn was just a smidge older, and if that was the reason he'd been lucky enough to lose both his front teeth right before school picture day.

Finn Michael Gustano, it said below the picture. *Born 3/4/11.*

"He has the same middle name as me?" Finn said, stunned. "And wait—does three-four mean March fourth?"

"He has the same name as you," Chess said, sounding dazed. "And the same birthday."

"And that Emma is Emma Grace, just like me," Emma added. She kept her gaze aimed at the screen, as if she was too surprised to look away. "And her birthday is April fourteenth, too."

"That's crazy," Finn said. "Weird, weird, weird. Did they just steal our names and birthdays? Or—I know." He yanked his hand away from Emma, put his fists on his hips, and tried to look stern. "Mom, did you let that other family clone us?"

He wanted everybody to laugh. He *needed* everybody to laugh. And then Mom would shut the laptop and forget those other kids; she would bring out snacks and ask Finn and Emma and Chess about school. Just like usual.

But Mom did none of those things. Even when Finn went over and snuggled against her, she didn't move.

She just kept staring at the kids who'd been kidnapped.

UNCOVER THE GREYSTONE SECRETS BY
MARGARET PETERSON HADDIX

"A satisfying narrative that portrays the complex anxieties and internal lives of close, caring family members grappling with a single set of extraordinary circumstances."

—*Publishers Weekly* (starred review)